OPERATION: AMAZON

WILLIAM MEIKLE

SEVERED PRESS
HOBART TASMANIA

OPERATION: AMAZON

Copyright © 2018 William Meikle
Copyright © 2018 by Severed Press

WWW.SEVEREDPRESS.COM

ISBN: 978-1-925840-21-6

-1-

"I'll give you this much, Cap," Wiggins said from the belly of the flat-bottomed boat, "you sure know how to show a girl a good time."

Captain John Banks swiped half a dozen lazy black flies away from his face, wiped sweat from his brow for the fourth time in as any minutes, and turned his gaze away from the river. Wiggins and McCally were in the process of brewing up a pot of tea on the portable solid fuel stove from the private's kit bag.

"What are you moaning about this time, Wiggo? I promised you something warmer, didn't I? It doesn't get much hotter than this."

"Warm shite is still shite," Wiggins said.

Banks laughed.

"Aye, I can't argue with that logic."

The flight into the Amazonian interior from the coastal airport had promised verdant greenery, shining waters, and a profusion of wildlife at first glance, but the bay they'd landed in had given Banks the first hint of what was in store for them on their trip upriver. Thick cloying mud banks lined the shores on both sides, choking the green out of the vegetation and leaving it gray and dead as far as 10 to 15 yards into the canopy. The river water was the color of milk chocolate—or warm watery shite as Wiggins would have it—as far as you could see. They'd transferred at the village from seaplane to fishing boat and now, with two river guides, were heading up the Amazon to their destination, slowly, through increasingly murky waters.

"I hope this shite doesn't get any thicker," McCally said, and once again Banks had to agree.

*

Like Wiggins, Banks had hoped for something warmer after Siberia.

"How do you fancy a jaunt to Brazil?" the colonel had said back in Lossiemouth almost 48 hours earlier, and Banks had almost bitten his superior's hand off to snatch at the job, before he'd even asked the nature of it. He had beaches and sun and Pina Colada in mind, and so had the squad when he'd gathered them for their briefing.

"I'll pack the sun-tan lotion and the Speedos," Wiggins had said, and Banks hadn't dissuaded them of their hopes of a cushy, warm, trip.

Instead, here they were in the depths of the Amazonian jungle, heading far upstream into the interior. They'd been motoring for hours, painfully slowly through what appeared little more than slurry, beset by all manner of flies, and sweating under thin camo-suits that were the only thing keeping them from being eaten alive by said insects.

"All in all, I'd rather be on a beach," Banks said, talking to himself, but Hynd heard him, and laughed.

"You and me both, Cap. So, it's a rescue mission, then?" the sergeant asked. He had a cigarette clamped in his mouth, and spoke with minimal movement of his lips. Smoke got in his eyes, causing them to water and giving him a squint, but it seemed to be keeping the worst of the flies away from him and, not for the first time, Banks considered returning to the old habit, if only for the relief from the biting flies.

"Maybe aye, maybe no," he replied, waving more of the black flies away from right in front of his nose. "I told you what the colonel told me—folks—engineers mainly—have been going missing from a dredging operation upriver; and some of them are British subjects. So we've got permission to go in and have a shufti. Whether anybody actually needs rescuing, we won't know until we get there and see what's what."

"And maybe we're only here to throw our weight around a bit, make a show to see if that puts a stop to any nonsense?" the sergeant said, smiling.

"Maybe aye, maybe no," Banks replied. "It wouldn't be the first time the colonel's had us resort to a bit of gunboat diplomacy."

"Why us, though, Cap?" McCally said from the belly of the boat. "There's any number of guys as well suited for a heavy mob job, and closer than we were."

Banks had held this last bit of info back for as long as possible, not having mentioned it in the briefing or on the long trip south, but they deserved to know.

"We've got form. There's talk that it might be some kind of animal attack. The colonel said he'd heard a rumor about a thing coming out of the jungle."

"Not more big fucking beasties," Wiggins said. "They should have sent for fucking Schwarzenegger and left us in peace." The private waved a hand out over the prow of the boat to the river. "And all this warm shite is coming downstream from the dredging operation? That's what we're here to protect?"

Banks nodded.

"Looks like you're shite monitor this week, Wiggo."

"What, again?" the private said. That got a laugh from the two guides behind them on the bench behind the small wheel on a pedestal that passed as the pilot's cabin area. The locals hadn't spoken much at their meeting in the village, only enough for Banks to know that they were getting well paid for the trip up river, and that they were father and son. On the boat trip so far, the two of them had stayed at the wheel at the rear of the long, low, boat under a tented canopy, smoking black cigarettes that even Hynd, a 40-a-day man given the opportunity, had turned down as too noxious.

The elder of the two and the owner of the boat, Giraldo, addressed Wiggins.

"You are Scottish, no?"

"I am Scottish, yes," Wiggins replied.

Giraldo's smile got broader.

"1982, World Cup. We kicked your boys in the ass. I watched it with my father and my uncles."

"That was a wee bit before my time," Wiggins replied. "But I've seen the highlights. At least we scored first."

"David Narey. Great goal," Giraldo replied. "But you just made my boys angry."

"You're a fitba' man then, Giraldo?" Wiggins asked.

"Man and boy," the guide replied. "And it is a great shame, but your football team is shit now, no?"

Wiggins laughed loudly.

"Our football team is shite now, yes," he said.

He moved up the boat and passed the guides each a mug of tea. He got some local smokes in reply, and Banks tuned the conversation out as it turned to the merits or otherwise of the respective national football teams. At least Wiggins was making friends though, for within minutes, the private and the two guides were thick as thieves.

"How long until we reach the dredging operation?" Wiggins asked.

"Two hours," Giraldo said, smiling. "Much more shite to see before then."

"Same as it ever was," Wiggins muttered.

*

Giraldo was spot-on in his estimation, although Banks knew they were getting close to their destination some time before they reached it; the water turned murkier, darker and thicker, until it both looked and felt like they were motoring through melted chocolate. The mud along the banks looked fresher here, wetter and still oozing but that only made it even less welcoming somehow.

Soon after the water turned thicker, they negotiated a wide bend in the river, and finally saw the full scale of the dredging operation laid out on the river ahead of them.

"It is a great blight," Giraldo said, sadness plain in his voice. "This used to be the perfect spot to catch enough fish for a month. But then these men with more money than sense came, and my fellow villagers could not refuse a pay that was many times more than they could make from the fishing. But look at the cost. Just look at it."

The main machine was housed on a flat structure the length and width of two football fields joined lengthwise. It seemed to be composed primarily of two parts—one machine for sucking up the riverbed, and another for filtering it, and throwing the resultant slurry wide across the river on either side. A dozen men worked on the flat deck, carting buckets to and from a deep pit of ooze for further filtering, at a guess, in trestles and tables that lined the center of the structure. The back end of the deck nearest to their approach housed a squat cube some 20 feet on a side that Banks guessed were the living quarters.

Giraldo brought them in directly at the rear, but even then they failed to avoid a misty spray of slurry that coated the boat, the squad and all their kit in a thin film of slimy mud that stank of rot and decay.

"I was right about the shite," Wiggins muttered as they came alongside a makeshift docking area.

They stepped quickly up and out of the boat, heaving their kit up onto the dredger's deck, where they were finally, thankfully, in an area clear of falling slurry, although Banks still tasted it in his throat.

A burly man came out of the cube, barrel-chested and squat, as brown as old mahogany in arms, face and legs, his shorts and shirt dark with slurry-muck, the only points of brightness being his blue eyes and the white of his teeth when he smiled.

He made straight for Banks and held out a hand.

"Captain Banks, I presume?" he said, his accent English, southern, and sounding strangely out of place here on the equatorial river.

"You're Buller?" Banks asked, and the man's smile faded quickly.

"No, I'm Joe the foreman, Joe Wilkes," he replied. "Buller's not here; and I need to talk to you about that. But not out here. Come inside; I have coffee and something to eat waiting."

As he turned away and Banks motioned the squad to follow him, six men, as mucky as Wilkes, but most definitely locals, walked quickly across the deck, passed the squad, and started talking, nearly shouting, to Giraldo. It was all in Portuguese, and too fast for Banks to catch any of it, but he recognized the look on the men's faces well enough; fear and he were old friends.

At the same time, one of the machines fell quiet around them and the wide arcs of slurry sputtered and died in a spatter of mud on the water.

"Get back to work," Wilkes said. "I didn't say you could stop."

The men around Giraldo ignored the Englishman, and kept up their worried flow of chat with the guide.

"I said get back to work," Wilkes said, louder, but again he was ignored. "You see what I'm dealing with?" he said to Banks, looking for an ally. Banks wasn't about to give him one just yet. There was more going on here than met the eye. Hynd had noted it too, but Banks stopped any questions with a finger to his lips, and turned back to follow Wilkes.

And hopefully get some answers.

*

The interior office Wilkes led them to inside the cube proved to be remarkably clean and cool, with a large air-conditioning unit by the only window to thank for the fresher air. They dropped their kit bags on the floor. Banks wiped at the thin slurry on his trousers, but only succeeded in spreading it around.

"The muck never really washes off," the foreman said apologetically, "but we do what we can to make ourselves comfortable. Beer or coffee?"

The squad was unanimous, and although there were nominally on duty, beer sounded exactly what Banks needed to get the taste of slurry from his mouth. When Wilkes disappeared down the corridor, then came back and handed out the bottles, it was cold, almost icy to the touch, hissed on opening, and it went down so fast it barely touched his throat.

It did the job he'd asked of it though, but he refused a second for him, and for the squad when Wilkes offered more

"Maybe later. But for now, tell me why Buller isn't here to meet us."

Wilkes lit up a smoke before answering, a cigar as thick as his thumb that took three matches to get going.

"The boss isn't here, and I don't know where he is," the foreman said. "He went last night, the same way as the others, quiet, in the night. This whole operation is fucked royally if you can't find him and get him back."

Banks saw that the big man was running on fumes, kept going by beer, smoke, and bravado in the face of something that had him terrified.

And if he's that worried, maybe I should be too.

"You'd better tell us the whole story," Banks said.

"In that case, I'll need another beer, and you'll need some grub. Through here."

He led them to a small refectory area, no more than a 10 by 10-foot square room lined with refrigerators and cupboards, with a low ceiling and a basic kitchen setup along the outside wall. It didn't have air conditioning, and the open windows let in heat, flies, and the rancid stench of the slurry. But the bread, meats, and cheeses on offer made up for any discomfort.

While the squad ate, Banks got a cup of strong coffee that tasted like it had been sitting for hours and sipped at it, and sat at a long trestle while he listened to Wilkes' story.

*

"Buller and I go back years," he started. "My first job out of University was working for his father in the Congo. Buller was on that rig as an assistant to the main boss man, but it was clear he was getting groomed for bigger things, so I hitched my wagon to his, and soon we both moved up the ranks. We were after oil that time in Africa but a river is a river, even a bloody big one like this, and we ironed out most of the kinks in the production process both there in the Congo then later in Jakarta, where it was silver we were after. Then Buller's old man got wind of small-scale prospectors making good money up here in the jungle and knew there was a fortune to be had if the operation could be scaled up properly. We started planning two years ago, then came the job of getting all the gear shipped up river and assembled.

"We've been dredging on the river for six months now," Wilkes continued. "At first, it all went like clockwork; we dredged, we sifted, and we found the gold we knew was lying there waiting to be brought up. The local lads on the team made more money than they'd see in years of fishing. We got to send pounds of gold back to be sold in the U.K. at an enormous markup. We're far enough away from the tree-huggers that nobody gives a fuck about any mess we might make, and the boss and his dad were happy as Larry.

"Things only changed when we came round that last bend and into this stretch of water. The local lads got twitchy, and although nothing was said to me, I would catch them in groups, muttering to each other, and it became obvious that they would stay near the center of the deck whenever they could, as if afraid of something in the water. And trying to get any of them to do anything after dark got to be near impossible, no matter how much I shouted, or how much money the boss offered them. Every minute of every day felt like we were on the edge of a full-blown mutiny.

"Then people started to disappear."

The big man stopped, and chewed at his cigar, his gaze taking on a far-away stare, the memory almost overwhelming him before he pulled himself together enough to continue.

"Jack Baillie was first to go—a Scots lad like you, field geologist and in charge of finding the best spots to dredge. He was a good laugh, a good chess opponent, and he was generally well liked by the local lads, for he kept up with them even when they were drinking their homemade rum.

"Then, one morning, he just wasn't there. There was no noise, no alarm. We got up for breakfast and he wasn't here. I went out in a boat, up and down the banks in case he'd maybe done something daft like gone for a swim after a drink, but there was no sign of any disturbance on either side, and no evidence of violence of any kind.

"There was a lot of nervous chatter among the men, but the boss offered double time pay for a few days if they'd allow it to be declared an accidental drowning. Money talks, even here in the fucking middle of nowhere, and nobody disagreed with Buller, and we went back to work.

"The second man went three nights later.

"This time, we heard the splash, but by the time we got to the side of the facility, there were only ripples in the water, and despite dredging the area, again no body was found. Even despite the boss' promise of even more cash, I damn nearly had a mutiny on my hands then. It was only Buller's talking about sackings and the prospect of losing their cash flow entirely that kept the men here.

"But now, with the boss going—and he went as quiet as Jack Baillie—now I don't think I can keep them here. Not unless you can help us."

*

It had all come out of Wilkes in a rush and, as if it had made him thirsty, he chugged a beer down in one, and then chewed hard at his cigar. Banks again saw the tension in the man, a bottled-up fear that might explode at any moment.

He was about to say something, a remark about how they'd do what they could to help, when there was a commotion in the corridor outside. Giraldo entered with his son and a small crowd of the deck workers at his back. Banks realized that everything else had gone totally quiet outside; all of the machines that ran the operation had been switched off completely and he couldn't feel the vibration that had been there, unnoticed underfoot until it was gone.

"I am taking these men home," Giraldo said, addressing Banks rather than the foreman. "If you wish, I will take you back now too. Otherwise, I will return for you, if you are still here."

Wilkes banged a fist hard on the table, and rose, anger suddenly blazing in him.

"They cannot leave."

Giraldo kept his gaze on Banks.

"They can, and they will. It is not safe here."

"They will get no more money, if that's what they're after," Wilkes shouted.

Giraldo smiled thinly.

"It is difficult to spend money when you are dead." He looked Banks in the eye. "I can take you back too?"

Banks shook his head.

"We stay. But we cannot stop you from leaving. Don't forget to come back, okay?"

"You will not be forgotten," Giraldo said, and put out a hand for Banks to shake. "Do not get dead before I return. Wiggins and I have much more football to discuss."

Banks saw that the fear of the workmen had spread to their guides, but also knew that the violence he felt thrum in the room might explode at any second. These men needed to leave, and any attempt to stop them would only make matters worse.

"Go then," he said, and Giraldo turned away. Wilkes looked ready to burst, and was about to grab for the guide, but Banks stopped him with a hand on his shoulder.

"It's for the best this way," he said. "We get to work without worrying about the safety of your crew, they get to come back when we get it sorted, and nobody else dies."

Wilkes still looked ready to argue, but Giraldo had already led the crew away, and minutes later, they all heard the thrum of the outboard as it left the dock and headed away back down the river.

The five men left in the refectory were now the only people remaining on board the dredger.

- 2 -

"That went well," Wiggins said laconically. They'd made their way back through to the relief of the air-conditioned office, and McCally had opened the kit bags.

"I thought so too," Banks replied. "At least we can get on with our business without distraction now. First things first. Sarge, you and Cally get first dibs. Tour the perimeter, don't lose sight of each other at any time, and Wiggo and I will join you at the door here in 20 minutes or so. Anything hinky, shoot first and ask questions later. Understood?"

Sergeant Hynd gave him a salute, retrieved his rifle and ammo from his kit bag, and left along with McCally to take the watch.

Banks turned to Wilkes. The man was opening a cupboard underneath where the laptop sat, and came out with a whisky bottle.

"Leave that alone," Banks said. "Maybe later, but for now, I need everybody clear-headed; even you. Do I know everything you know?"

"I told you. Everybody went so quiet, so quickly, there's nothing to know apart from the fact that they all fucked off without anybody noticing. And I'm worried that I might be next, so if you're here to help, start helping."

"And there's really nothing else?"

"Apart from sharing the local superstitions, which are local, and superstitions, I've told you everything," Wilkes replied.

Banks saw the truth in the man's open, almost pleading, gaze. He wasn't going to get much more than he already knew.

But I need more.

"Okay, what about a guess then? In your opinion, where would be the best place for us to start looking for your boss?"

Wilkes stood and went over to a large map on the wall. He traced the river further upstream with his finger, and jabbed at a spot to the west of their current position.

"I'd start here," he said. "It's higher ground, and rough terrain. It's also where most of the gold gets washed down from, and where we're ultimately headed once we've cleaned out the riverbed. And it's an open secret about the source of the gold. I've heard a rumor, through Buller's old man, that there's a German outfit trying to get there first, and it's my guess, my professional opinion if you like, that it's them that's causing us all this grief. Industrial sabotage, for want of a better term. They'll have the missing men holed away somewhere," he tapped the map again, "somewhere around here."

"There's been no ransom demands?"

Wilkes shook his head. It was all the reply needed. Banks went over to look at the area on the map. There were no roads marked, no settlements, only higher ground and snaking tributaries.

"Does anybody live out there?"

"Not that I know of," Wilkes said. "There's some chat of a curse among the workers but that's more of their superstitious bollocks."

Banks turned from the map.

"Okay then—how do we get there?"

"Your guide's boat is the best bet, you know, the one you let him leave in. Failing that, we've got three canoes tied up front, but there are no outboards and paddling against the current would be a bastard of a job all the way."

"A bastard of a job you say?" Wiggins replied with a smile. "In my experience, we never get any other kind."

Banks gave the private a look that shut him up fast, then turned back to Wilkes.

"How long would it take us to get up there?"

Wilkes shrugged and showed his open palms.

"I'm no expert, but in the canoes? Four hours maybe, and you'd be faster coming back with the current in your favor."

"And it'll be at least six before our guide gets back here?" Banks said, calculating the return trip of the one they'd just made.

"If he bothers to come back at all," Wilkes replied and went back to the desk, reaching for the whisky bottle again and pouring a three-finger measure into a tumbler. This time, Banks didn't stop the man as he knocked it back in one smooth motion and poured another.

Banks turned back to Private Wiggins.

"Gear up, Wiggo," he said. "Let's go find these canoes."

"Up shite creek again, cap?" Wiggins replied.

"Aye," Banks said. "But at least we'll have a paddle."

*

They met Hynd and McCally outside by the rear docking area. Banks brought everybody up to speed and outlined the plan while the other three men had a smoke to try to keep the flies at bay.

"It's only a reccy mission for now," he said. "I want to get a look upstream a way, so we'll take two canoes out for a paddle. It'll be minimal kit for now. We go tooled up, but leave the bulk of our gear here with Wilkes and travel light; water, guns, and ammo only. I intend to be back here in time for our guide's return, so fast and quiet is the order of the day. Let's get going."

As they walked up the center of the flat deck, Hynd pointed out what he and the corporal had seen on their inspection of the perimeter.

"What does it all do?" Banks asked.

Hynd waved a hand to the left, then right.

"That's a fucking huge sucking thing that chews up the riverbed below us, and that's a big blowing thing that sends all the shite flying to the banks," Hynd said. "At least, that's Cally's opinion. But you ken how he is with technical terminology. Apart from the filters, which are also fucking huge, there doesn't seem to be a lot else to it. And there's no sign of any foul play; in fact, no sign of anything untoward at all to report."

"Let's hope we find something up river," Banks replied. "It's a fucking big jungle to lose somebody in."

Hynd jerked a thumb back toward the living quarters.

"What about Wilkes?"

"He's got a bottle, and a cigar. I doubt he'll get out of his chair before we get back. It's his boss we're here to find."

"Will you call it in?"

Banks tapped at the pocket at his chest where he kept the sat-phone.

"Maybe later. The first thing the colonel will ask is if we've done a reccy. So we'll do a reccy, then get back and hope there's some whisky left in that bottle."

*

The canoes sat low in the water and were longer and thinner than the single person vessels which Banks was more used to. But it felt stable on the water, and very maneuverable once they coordinated their paddling effectively. With two men in each, front and rear, and both paddling, they made quicker time than Banks had expected, and were soon round a long bend, out of sight of the dredging operation, and into a different world entirely.

Here away from the rain of slurry that had cloyed and choked the banks downstream, the trees, green and vibrant, almost luminescent, crowded down to, and into, the water. The river flowed, not brown but a deep blue, crystal clear and the water was filled with a bewildering array of fish in all sizes and colors. Dragonflies as big as sparrows darted over the surface and every few seconds there would be a splash as a fish rose for lunch. Higher up in the canopy, birds screeched and something heavier which might have been a monkey or sloth caused large broad leaves to rain down into the water to float away like discarded umbrellas.

The sun beat down hard from a cloudless sky and heat washed off the river in waves that had sweat running in a film inside Banks' suit. Although they were making good time on the water, he knew that hours of paddling in this heat was out of the question. It had only been fifteen minutes so far, and already he felt his strength ebbing away.

"How far do you mean to go, Cap?" Wiggins asked from up front, and Banks saw that, like himself, the private was already flagging. He knew the men would keep going until they dropped if he asked them to. But he also knew he shouldn't be asking them to.

"A wee bit farther," he called out, to ensure they'd hear him in the other canoe. "But we won't make much headway in this heat, so 10 more minutes of this shite, then we'll turn back."

He heard the relief in Wiggins' voice.

"Righty-ho, Cap."

The slight surge of the canoe told him that the private had put a bit more effort into his stroke, now that he knew there was an imminent end in sight, and Banks followed suit. They cut through the water faster than before, but it didn't get them any difference in the view to either side; there was still only the wall of green, like a solid barrier between river and sky. After the 10 minutes were up, he'd seen enough. As there was no possibility of getting anywhere near the higher ground marked on the map, and nothing to gain by trying and failing, he opted for a strategic retreat until they didn't have to make the trip under their own power.

"That's far enough. Hang a left, Wiggo," he said loudly. "We'll let the current help us back downstream."

At almost the same time, McCally shouted out from the other canoe.

"Hang on. There's something in the water up ahead, coming this way."

Banks and Wiggins pulled their canoe up alongside the other, and watched as McCally leaned over and scooped something out of the water. The corporal held it up, still dripping, and showed them a zip-locked plastic bag, puffed up with air so that it would float. There was what looked like a recent model cellular phone inside it.

"Well, there's something you don't see every day," Wiggins said.

Banks took the package from the corporal. The screen of the phone was blank, and stayed that way when he tried to switch it on through the clear bag.

"We can hope it's only the battery needing charging," he said, and slid the package inside his shirt. "Fuck knows who it belongs to or why it's floating about on the river. But that's a mystery we're not going to solve out here—unless there's more weird shite coming down to us?"

They held position in the same spot long enough for the squad to have a rest and a smoke, only having to paddle lightly to maintain position in a calmer spot near the left side bank. They kept a close eye on the water, but nothing else came down the river and once the smokes were done and the stubs sent hissing into the water, Banks gave the order to turn and head back for the dredger.

- 3 -

The journey back took less than half the time and they only had to paddle enough to keep them in the fastest part of the current. Even then, the heat sapped what little strength they had left, and Banks was glad to glance up and see that they were on the last bend before the facility's position.

Once they navigated the river bend, Banks looked toward the dredger, almost hoping to see their guide's boat moored at the rear dock, but the whole operation sat as quiet and dead as it had been when they'd left. It would be some hours yet before they could realistically hope for the boat's return.

"I hope Wilkes has saved us a beer," Wiggins said. "I'm bloody gasping here."

Banks shared the sentiment; his shoulders and arms felt heavy as stones and every breath was like breathing in steam; they were going to need the guide's boat if they wanted to penetrate deeper upriver. And the finding of the phone had now made that a priority rather than a possibility, for Banks had already made a good guess as to its owner.

*

After docking, they walked quickly back to the living quarters where, to Banks' surprise, they found Wilkes, still sober, and preparing a pot of fish stew in the mess area.

"We expected to find you pished on the floor," Wiggins said.

"We're not all Scotsmen. The whisky is back in the cupboard," Wilkes replied with a wry grin. "I only had what you saw me take. Purely medicinal, I assure you."

"Aye, well I might take some of that medicine myself later," Banks replied. "But first, do you have any beer left?"

"Oh, we have plenty of that," he replied. "We run out of fuel before we ever run out of beer."

Wilkes went to a fridge and came out with a six-pack of beer that the squad took gratefully. Banks rubbed the cold bottle against his cheek as he took the zip-locked packet from inside his shirt and passed it across to Wilkes.

"Is this his?" he said. They both knew who Banks had referred to, and Wilkes nodded, suddenly agitated.

"He bought it new on his last trip home. It's his pride and joy. You didn't find him, did you? Tell me he's not dead."

Banks took the packet and handed it to McCally.

"We only found the phone," he replied. "My corporal here will see what he can get from it. All we know is that it came down, in the plastic packet, from somewhere farther upstream."

"Maybe it's meant as a message," Wilkes said eagerly.

"And maybe he lost it accidentally," Banks replied. "Let's not be jumping to any conclusions here. All we can say at the moment is that it came from upstream."

*

"I got a couple of minutes of video off the phone's card," McCally said when he called them through to the office 10 minutes later. "I've hooked up the laptop, so gather round. But I warn you, it's weird shite."

They all gathered close as McCally started the recording running,

The video started up in darkness, then a face came into focus, lit only by whatever feeble light was coming from the camera screen, throwing pitch-black shadow around nostrils and eye sockets and giving the face the look of a bone-white skull.

"Is that Buller?" Banks said.

"Yep, that's him," Wilkes replied. "But what the hell is he playing at?"

McCally had the sound turned up to full volume, but even then they needed to bend in even closer to hear as the man spoke, barely more than a whisper. Terror was plain though, in every word of the Scotsman's speech.

"I don't know how long I've got, and I can only thank fuck I had a sample pouch in my pocket, so I'm going to send this out the window in a minute or so, and hope it gets to somebody that can do something about it."

The man was clearly nervous, his eyes wide, blinking rapidly. The phone shook in his hand, and Banks was immediately reminded of a terrible shaky-cam horror movie that Wiggins and McCally made him sit through on a night off in Inverness.

Is this some kind of candid-camera con? If it's somebody's idea of a joke, they're going to get a bullet up their arse.

Banks turned his attention fully to the screen as Buller continued.

"I have no idea where the fuck I am or how the fuck I got here. I went to sleep in my bed; and the dreams were delirious, fucked-up nonsense, so I assume I was drugged. I woke up here, feeling like a badger has shat in my mouth and with my head birling. 'Here' is somewhere high up; the air is fresh, cooler than down on the river, and I hear running water, a cascade, like a waterfall. I'm in some old stone building, Mayan at a guess, and as far as I can tell, I'm facing south. Now you know as much as I do.

Just fucking come and get me. Please?"

The frightened face looked away from the screen, then back again.

"Shite, somebody's coming."

The view swung wildly, the soundtrack cracking and rustling, and then the picture went slightly opaque, as if being seen through smoke. Banks realized that the phone had now been placed inside the zip-lock bag. The voice started up again, even more muffled than previously.

"Here goes nothing. Out the window with you, and I hope to fuck you get somewhere. Come and get me. Please?"

At the last second, before the screen went dark and quiet, they caught a glimpse back into the room from which the phone had been thrown. McCally used the mouse to quickly stop the video, and clicked twice through the frames until they had the one with the best view of the room. They clearly saw the man who'd thrown the phone, standing at a tall open window in a stone wall. Behind him, deep in shadow and coming through a doorway, was—something—it didn't look human, although the shadows were such that it was hard to tell much of anything. If Banks had to bet on it, he'd have said it was a snake, but given the size of the room and the distance from the camera, it was a snake that had a head more than a foot wide between the eyes.

*

Everyone around the laptop fell quiet, trying to take in what they'd seen. McCally showed no sign of moving the mouse to control the video, which was stuck showing that last frame.

"Is that it?" Banks asked the corporal.

"That's all the video I could find," McCally said. "But the phone's a smart wee fucker. There's a built-in GPS that's been saving data on where the phone has been when it's switched on.

It's not always had a signal, and it's patchy at best, but there's two points on the map that are clear enough, each being saved half a dozen times at least." He went over to the large map and pointed. "One's here, on the river where we are now. The other's here."

Banks went over to check the spot that McCally's finger now covered. It was a high area of ground, in the highlands to the north, the same area that Wilkes had pointed out to him earlier.

The job had now definitely become a rescue mission.

-4-

"We cannae get the canoes all the way up there, Cap," Hynd said. "Not all in one trip anyway. We were knackered after less than half an hour earlier, and yon's a good four hours of paddling at least. We'd be fit for fuck all by the time we got there, if we got there at all."

Banks agreed, but they had no idea how long their guide might take to return, and the thought of their mission, now a possible hostage retraction, worried at him. The squad retired to the mess for Wilkes' stew and then a smoke break, but Banks sat at the laptop, playing the snippet of video over and over, hoping to see some fresh clue that might have eluded him. Then, when no inspiration came, and he knew he couldn't put it off any longer, he called in on the sat-phone, making his first report to the colonel back in Lossiemouth.

"S1, checking in," he said when the call was answered. He heard the usual whirrs and clicks as the call was scrambled and put through to his superior's desk. He realized, too late, that it was going to be very late evening back in Scotland, but the colonel answered immediately at the other end.

"Are we ready to bring the package home?" he asked.

From there on, it went about as well as Banks could have expected. His superior officer listened, went quiet for several breaths, then spoke, his crisp tones coming through more than clear enough to be understood.

"Buller is the mission," he said. "Everybody else is either hostile or expendable, but bring Buller home however you can. Understood?"

"Understood, sir," Banks replied.

"Check back in 24 hours from this mark," the colonel said. "I expect good news."

Hynd came in as Banks finished the call, and put a bowl of stew and a cold beer on the table.

"Eat up, Cap," the sergeant said, "before Cally and Wiggo polish it off between them."

The fish stew was strangely spiced and tasted faintly of the muck of the riverbed, but with the help of the beer, it went down well enough. It did a lot to get back some of the strength that had been sapped by the heat and the effort of paddling earlier.

"Orders, Cap?" Hynd asked.

"We go after Buller," Banks said, "and we've got a day to get him out of here—the boss was feeling generous."

"The lads will take to the paddling, if you ask them," Hynd said.

"I know," Banks said. "But I'm of a mind to wait for Giraldo and some power to get us upriver. Keep the lads off the booze for a couple of hours until the boat's back here. Wilkes too. We might need to know something that he knows, so make sure he's sober."

Hynd saluted, then nodded toward the screen, where Banks had stopped it again on that final, inexplicable image.

"What are we up against here, Cap?"

"I've not got a clue," Banks replied. "Some daft bugger in a rubber suit, or a real big fucking snake, it hardly matters either way. We've got our orders, and we'll find out soon enough one way or the other."

*

Giraldo returned right about when Banks expected him to. He was alone in the boat when they met it at the rear dock.

"I left my boy with the others," the guide said as he tied up the boat. "There is no sense in us both being in danger. Can we go now?"

"I'm afraid not," Banks said. "We paid you to get us where we need to go. And where we need to go is further upstream."

The guide went pale, and paler still when Banks took him inside to the laptop and showed him the video playback. The man crossed himself, twice, and muttered something. It was in Latin, not Portuguese, and Banks guessed it was a prayer.

Giraldo looked into Banks' eyes.

"It is as your Mister Wiggins would say, 'bad shite,' Captain. You do not wish to go to that place if you do not need to."

"We need to," Banks said, pointing to the screen. "One of our countrymen is being held there."

"He is most certainly already dead, or wishes he was," the guide said, with such certainty that Banks felt it sink into his own heart as truth.

"Nevertheless, we will go, and we will go now. We can take your boat anyway, but I'd rather have you with us, for you know the river and its ways. But if you want, you can stay here with Wilkes. We will be back in the morning, one way or the other."

The guide didn't reply, but Wilkes spoke at Banks' back.

"I'm coming with you," he said. "Buller's my boss, but he's also my friend. I'm coming."

Giraldo spoke up.

"And you cannot have my boat without me," he said, the resignation clear in his voice. "So I will take you. You will need me on the river in any case, for it can be treacherous enough by day, let alone by night. But promise me one thing, Captain,"

'Name it," Banks said.

Giraldo did a fair impression of Wiggins.

"If you see anything shite, shoot the fuck out of it first, and ask questions later."

*

Banks had the squad get kitted up.

"Night goggles, ammo, rifles, and water. Leave everything else here. I've got a hunch that hard and fast is going to be the only way this one will get done."

Five minutes later, they were all in Giraldo's boat, the outboard taking them around the side of the dredger and onto the open river, making far better time than they had in the canoes earlier. Banks looked back, and saw the lights of the living quarters glowing bright against the background of mud on the banks; dusk was approaching fast. Banks welcomed it, for darkness would give them cover for the forthcoming operation.

The squad sat in the middle area of the boat, Wilkes with them, all getting smokes lit. Banks moved back to join Giraldo, for the tang of tobacco was starting to remind him again of how much he missed the old habit. He stepped back and joined their guide at the wheel, sitting beside him on the rickety bench that passed as the captain's seat.

"Thank you for agreeing to this," Banks said. "I owe you a favor."

"I would not let any man take this journey alone who did not need to, but I do not like this, Captain," Giraldo said. "We never go this far up river; not even for the fishing."

"Why not?"

Giraldo shook his head.

"You would not believe me. You would think me a superstitious native; Mister Buller certainly thought that of me. Wilkes here still thinks that of me."

"I am not Buller or Wilkes," Banks said, and, remembering Antarctica and the high weirdness the squad had seen, and fought, in that cold Nazi bunker, pressed the question. "Try me. I too have seen things that would make you think me a superstitious native."

Giraldo thought he was being teased and looked him straight in the eye for a long time, then Banks saw recognition in the man's stare.

"I believe you have, Captain." He poured them each a mug of thick, black coffee from a battered thermos and handed it to Banks, then lit up one of his noxious black cigarettes before continuing.

"It is a story we are all told as children in the village. I had it from my father, who had it from his father before him and so on, as far back as there have been fish in the river and men to catch them. I know now, having told it to my own boy, that it is a cautionary tale. It is meant to stop our young ones from venturing too far onto the river alone. But I also know there to be more than a kernel of truth in it. As to how I know this, I might tell you that too, but first, the story, as I heard it that first day I was old enough to take to the water."

He began the tale in the singsong voice common to all such stories everywhere.

*

"Long ago, when the world was yet young and there were more fish than water in the river, there lived a boy in a village on the south bank.

"Raul was a boisterous child, always looking far away from his duties to hearth and home. His father tried to get him to work in the forest or on the river, but at the end of each day the work was not done, and Raul was found, ever more distant from his village, exploring the dark byways of the water.

"Every day he would venture farther. He began taking light

with him, in order to see the dark places better, carrying flint and straw to make firebrands that he would carry on his explorations.

"It was during one such exploration, farther from his village than he had ever been, that he found the cave, a black cavern that ran deep into a rocky outcrop in the upper reaches of the river where it approaches the mountains where the gods live. He lit a fresh brand, his hands trembling with excitement as he did so, and ventured inside.

"His young head was full of the thought of treasure, of the ancient gold so sought after by the Conquistadors that they had marched into the jungle in their thousands after it, never to be seen again. Raul was not worried about suffering such a fate—he had his fire to lead him and warm him in the darkness.

"The cave went down deep into the hill, so far that all light from outside was lost, and there was only the burning brand. But still Raul for not afraid, for his burning curiosity was stronger than any fear. Panic only fluttered in his chest when he turned a corner, and stepped into a far larger, cavernous chamber. Something gleamed there in the dark, flickering golden in reply to his own fire. A voice spoke from the shadows, old beyond time, weary beyond sleep, as loud as thunder in the blackness.

"'I like your red eye, boy,' the voice said. 'Give it to Boitata. She will take care of it for you.'

"Raul turned to flee but a great wind, warm as fire, blew through the cave, and blew out his brand as simply as puffing out a candle. He was left alone there in the deepest dark.

"But that wasn't the worst thing. The worst thing was the fiery red eyes that opened, and blinked at him, tens, scores, hundreds of them there in the dark, coming closer as Boitata slithered from her sleep."

*

"Back in the village, Raul's father was frantic with worry as darkness fell, for young Raul was nowhere to be found. The father took to the river in his canoe, going up and down the banks and calling the boy's name, but still there was no reply, and darkness was coming quickly. The man was making a turn for home when he heard it, a great splash in the water, and a surge under the boat as something huge swam beneath him. There came another splash, and suddenly Raul was there, splashing frantically in the water and crying most piteously. His father dragged the boy aboard, and at the same time Boitata came up out of the water, rising up high above the canoe and looking down, deliberately showing the father what had been done before sinking back into the river.

"The canoe went still in the water again as the father bent over the boy, looking down at his face, and the black, empty holes where his eyes had been. He did not need to ask the whimpering child what had happened—he had already seen for himself. The last thing he had been shown before Boitata sank back into the river had been Raul's eyes, now showing flecks of fiery red, looking back at him from the great head of the river serpent."

- 5 -

Banks almost applauded; the man had put everything into the story, and Banks had been rapt and lost in it as if he too had been a child in the village at the knees of an elder. Giraldo smiled in return and lit another cigarette. Banks waited to see if more was coming, but the guide fell quiet, watching the river ahead.

"You said there was more?" Banks said when it was clear the man would need prompting.

Giraldo wasn't smiling when he replied.

"There is more, yes. But that part of the tale is not a story I want to tell on this stretch of the river, in the dark, Captain," he replied. "There is only a certain amount of tempting fate with which I am comfortable, and I believe I have reached my limit for the night. Besides, the river can get tricky around these parts, and I need my full concentration on the water. If we are still here, still alive in the morning, when the sun is full, I shall share a beer and my story with you, so you can count that as a promise."

"I will hold you to it," Banks replied, then left the man alone to do his job.

*

The squad still sat in the middle of the boat, smoking and brewing up a pot of tea on the camp stove. Banks squeezed past them, carefully making his way forward so as not to set the vessel rocking, and went up front to join Wilkes where the big man sat beside a pair of large floodlights that showed the way ahead. A myriad of small white fish roiled and leapt at the prow as if trying to catch the light, and moths the size of Bank's palms fluttered and swarmed around the lamps. Every so often a dark shape, bats as big as crows, would swoop among the insects and carrying one off in the black as quickly as it had come. Over by the left-hand bank, a pair of large, pale-yellow eyes blinked twice, but the boat had motored past before Banks properly recognized them as belonging to an alligator that had to be at least 10 feet long nose to tail. Now that the heat of the day was fading, the jungle and its inhabitants were much more alive.

It was almost full dark now, and the light showed only 10 to 15 yards ahead of them on the water. Everything else was mostly deep blackness and thick shadows; Banks had no idea how Giraldo was navigating, but he was rapidly developing a sense of admiration for the man's skill, and not only in his storytelling ability.

"How do you like our river now, Captain?" the big man said.

"I like this boat. It's better than paddling, I'll give you that," Banks said, and Wilkes laughed.

"Then again, anything's better than paddling," the big man replied. "But we're making good time. We should be near the highlands in an hour or so. Do you have a plan?"

It was Banks' turn to laugh.

"To quote my private, the plan's as simple as shite. We go in, we find our man, we get out, and we shoot the fuck out of anything that gets in our way."

"Works for me," Wilkes said. He patted at his hip, and for the first time, Banks noted that the man had a handgun holstered there. He resolved to make sure Wilkes was kept far away from any possible action. The last thing he needed was for an amateur to get involved in any firefight.

*

Wilkes' prediction of their arrival time proved to be right, almost to the minute. After an hour of cruising in the dark, Giraldo took them in a sharp turn to the left into an inlet and a minute after that the lights picked out a stone quay directly ahead of them, high enough that it loomed above their heads, even when they stood up. As the boat slowed to approach the structure, the lights brought it into sharp relief. Banks saw that the stones from which the quay was built were ancient in the extreme. They had been badly corroded by the river and weather and smoothed to a polish by the current in places, encrusted with freshwater barnacles and algae up to two feet above the water line in other spots. But the whole thing was built with such precision that the wall itself had stood obdurate against the Amazon for centuries, perhaps millennia.

As Giraldo brought the boat around to moor parallel to the wall, Banks also saw that each brick was so tightly packed against its neighbors that there was no sign of any mortar. He'd seen such work before, in megalithic tombs on Orkney and Malta, and in the great temples of Egypt. He had not expected to find it here, in the upper reaches of the jungles of the Amazon.

It seemed, however, that Giraldo knew the place, for he brought the boat to a halt tight up close to a ledge and a set of stone steps that led directly up to the top of the wall of the quay. He cut the engine and quickly tied them up to a stone pillar set on the steps.

"I stay here with the boat," Giraldo said. It wasn't a question, and in truth, Banks was glad he didn't have to persuade the guide otherwise.

"Wilkes will stay with you," Banks replied. "I'm not leaving you here alone."

The big man looked like he might argue, but one look from

Banks was enough to keep him quiet.

"I'm trusting you here, Wilkes," Banks said. "We might need to make a quick getaway, so you're our backup plan. Just hang out here, and don't do anything stupid. We'll be back before you know it."

That seemed to be enough to mollify any resentment Wilkes had been carrying, and the big man threw Banks a mock salute in reply.

"You've been here before?" Banks asked Giraldo.

"Only this far and no more," the guide said. "I did not go ashore, and I did not stay long."

There was more to it, Banks saw it in the guide's eyes and his manner, but he didn't have time to probe any deeper. It would have to wait. He waved a hand above the quay, away from the river and under the tall canopy of foliage.

"How far will we have to walk?"

Giraldo shrugged.

"The ground rises quickly, I remember that much. And there is a building, a tower of a sort, higher up on the hill. But as to where they might be holding Mister Buller? That is anyone's guess."

"So, a walk in the jungle, at night, with no idea where we're headed?" Wiggins said. "This shite gets thicker by the minute."

*

Banks turned back to Giraldo while the squad got geared up.

"Do you have a flare gun?"

The guide nodded.

"In a box under the wheel."

"If there's any sign of trouble, send one up. Hopefully we'll see it, and come running."

Banks checked his gear; he had his rifle, spare magazines of ammo in a vest over his jacket, and a pair of night goggles that he pulled down and set to full intensity as he stepped out of the boat and up the steps onto the quay. A quick look around told him he was alone, with a wall of jungle ahead of him. A stone walkway, little more than a yard wide, led off to his left away from the river, through a gap in the foliage.

"All clear. Move out, lads," Banks said. "Remember, we're going in hard and fast. Don't fuck up."

He turned to wait for the squad to come out of the boat and up the steps to join him.

"Give us four hours, tops," he said to Wilkes and Giraldo. "After that, feel free to head back down river; if we're not back by then, we're probably not coming any time soon."

The squad all stepped up onto the quay, awaiting orders. Banks pointed them toward the stone track leading into the jungle.

"Looks like we go that way," he said. "Sarge, you take point. Wiggo, watch our backs. Move out."

Hynd led them away toward the track. Banks had a last look back; the lamps of Giraldo's boat were blinding bright in the night goggles, but he saw the man's wave clear enough. He waved back, then followed Hynd and McCally into the jungle.

*

The goggles made the surrounding jungle appear even greener, almost luminescent. Foliage hemmed them in and it felt like walking inside a vast glistening tube, the intestine of a green fleshy giant. The humidity was stifling, and heavy with a dampness that made breathing a chore. Every step moved a film of sweat around under kit, and the eye goggles slid as moisture ran down his forehead from his hairline. Small animals scurried in the dark just out of sight, and overhead, parakeets fluttered noisily at their passing.

We might as well have rung the fucking doorbell.

Banks was glad when the track took a turn to the right and they climbed upward, out from under the canopy. The parakeets settled quickly back in their roosts and the night once again fell quiet save for the pad of their footsteps on the stone underfoot.

The path now made its way up the side of a rocky hill. The growth was less luxuriant here, and a light breeze, although warm, meant that the humidity fell to an almost acceptable level, and every so often they got a view back downward, to where the canopy seemed to stretch off endlessly. The river snaked away to their right, shimmering green and silver. The quay they'd left behind was hidden under the canopy, and Banks could only hope that it was a quiet enough spot that Giraldo and Wilkes would not need to use their emergency flares.

And with that, he put the boat and the other two men out of his mind; his focus now had to be on the path ahead, and the mission. He looked up instead of down. The path was climbing, slowly, around the outside of a long hill whose top was lost in the dark somewhere higher up.

They passed more stone workings as they climbed, more proof as to the antiquity of the builders. At first, it was only small rounded dwelling huts, long since collapsed into ruin and overgrown with moss, lichen, and vine, making them almost appear as natural aspects of the landscape rather than anything built by man. As they went higher, and after 10 minutes of strenuous climbing, the ruins became less sporadic. After a short, steeper set of worn steps, they passed through what had obviously been a gateway at one long lost time, and the path widened and flattened out, becoming more of a street, wending its way, still upward, through the tumbled ruins of an ancient town.

The rounded design of the dwellings was still evident here, but here they were more tightly packed together, almost butting right up against one another. The doorways were dark, in deep shadow, and the tumbled ruins jutted into the sky like shattered teeth. There was no sign of any life save a pair of pale doves that fluttered up and away in panic at their approach.

Once they were sure that the sudden flight of the birds hadn't alerted anyone to their presence, McCally slowed to let Banks catch him, and spoke in a whisper.

"Who the fuck built all of this, Cap? I thought it was nowt but jungle around here?"

Banks had been thinking the same thing. His knowledge of ancient peoples was sketchy at best; he knew the names, Aztec, Inca, and one other.

"It's probably Mayan, at a guess," he said. "But don't quote me on that, as I think we've fucked up enough already. Look around, Cally. This is bloody ancient. Nobody's lived here for centuries. I think we've come to the wrong place. Our man's not here."

The next few minutes only seemed to harden Bank's belief that they were on a wild goose chase. The path flattened out as they walked onto the hilltop, a plateau where the bulk of the town had been. Although the buildings were of a larger scale up here on the ridge, the whole site looked to be mostly a jumble of tumbled, overgrown ruin and Banks was losing hope. Then Hynd stopped abruptly and motioned them into cover behind a partially fallen wall before waving Banks forward.

"Light ahead, Cap," the sergeant whispered when Banks joined him at the wall.

Banks lifted his goggles up onto his brow and chanced a quick look round the edge. There was just about enough light by the stars to give him a clear view. They were at one end of a long causeway that ran all the way along the ridge. Buildings lined either side of a main thoroughfare that must have been grand and monumental at one time, but was now mostly a tumble of ruins and crawling vines. The largest structure of note that still stood complete faced him at the far end of the ridge, some 100 yards away, a squat, stepped pyramid. The light Hynd had mentioned came from an entrance way atop the line of steps, a yellow-gold flickering that Hynd guessed must be firebrands or some kind of lantern.

And now they had stopped, he heard something that had not been audible earlier, having been masked by their footsteps. There was a rush of water in the distance, coming from the same direction as the pyramid. He remembered Buller's video message, and the mention of a cascade and his hope rose again; perhaps they had come to the right spot after all.

He turned back to Hynd and spoke softly.

"Up the center of the main drag," he said. "Two by two, eyes on each flank. You and Cally go first. If we make it that far without any fuss, we go up the steps and see where that light's coming from. Everybody got it?"

The three other men replied in the affirmative.

Hynd and McCally moved them out.

- 6 -

The road was paved underfoot, six-foot square gray slabs, some cracked with age but for the most part in good enough condition to drive a cart along should it be required, although there was no sign that anyone had done so for many years. Banks watched the shadows amid the ruins, expecting an attack at any moment. None came. The only sound was once again the pad of their footsteps on stone, accompanied by the soft rush of water running away in the distance. He kept his goggles on his forehead. The sky was a shimmering blanket of stars overhead, with no moon to dim its brilliance, and with that, and the flickering light atop the pyramid showing them the way, there was more than enough light for their purposes.

They reached the base of the pyramid without anyone taking notice of them and looked up. The steps were each a foot or more high, and the structure was larger than it had looked from the other end of the causeway, stretching high above then toward the field of stars. Banks saw Wiggins eyeing the climb warily.

"Up you go, Wiggo," he said. "Let's see how far you get before you run out of puff."

"That's what the sarge's wife says too," the man replied and was climbing up and away before Hynd got a chance to reply. Banks let McCally and Hynd go ahead and brought up the rear as they headed up the steps.

*

It proved to be hard work and despite the fact it was cooler now than under the height of the sun, Banks still had a new film of sweat under his suit before they were even halfway to the top. At least here in the fresher air they were spared the worst of the biting insects and, as they rose higher, he got some idea as to why the pyramid and surrounding complex had been built where it was. The high vantage gave them a view over an endless swathe of forest, and the river, dark as pitch with highlights picked out by reflected stars, a vast snake slithering far below them.

When he stopped to draw a breath, he heard the cascade again, louder now, closer, off to his right on the far side of the pyramid somewhere. But there were no windows on this face of the structure. If their rescue were to be successful, they'd have to venture inside to find the man they'd come for. Banks felt the old tingle of anticipation rise in him, and after boating, canoeing and hiking all this way, he was about ready for any action that might come his way.

He turned and looked up the steps to where the flickering yellow light called them forward. The other three were already four steps higher, so Banks put some effort into it to catch up, and felt the strain in his calves. By the time he reached the top, one step behind the others, he was sweating again, and breathing heavily. Wiggins laughed.

"Who's out of puff now, Cap?"

Banks smiled back.

"Just for that, you get to go first, Wiggo."

*

They all turned toward the source of the flickering light. It was an open-arched entrance into 10 feet on a side cube that sat directly on the top of the pyramid. Three wall sconces, crude oil lamps, burned at eye height. They lit an altar that sat in the center of the room, and threw shadows across a passageway on the far side that appeared to lead away onto darkness.

A pale body lay on the altar, and Banks thought that their rescue was over before it really got started, but as he stepped in after Wiggins, he saw that it wasn't the man they had seen on the video. It wasn't Buller, but Wilkes had spoken of other men being taken, and Banks guessed this must be one of them, a beardless, thin chap, thinner still now due to his belly being open and his insides having been hollowed out. It hadn't been done recently, for the blood was brown and crusted where it had run down the altar stone. The body was severely abused, in particular where the rib cage had been cracked and splayed. Banks didn't look too closely, but that too appeared hollowed out, the body little more now than an empty shell where a man had been.

Somebody's here all right. And they'll pay for this butchery.

"What's this now then?" Wiggins said. "Some kind of ancient torture shite?"

"Ritual, more like," Hynd replied. "A sacrifice, I'd guess."

"A sacrifice to what though?" Wiggins asked. "What kind of fucking god demands this kind of wet work as tribute?"

"Most kinds of fucking gods, in my experience," Hynd replied and spat at the base of the altar. He turned to Banks.

"The guide might be right, you know? Our man might be dead already," he said.

Banks was eyeing the dark corridor on the far side of the chamber. He pulled his goggles down over his eyes and stepped around the altar to the shadowed entranceway.

"Dead or alive, he's coming back with us. I've had enough of this shite already. Let's get this done. There's beer back in the fridge on the dredger, and I'm getting awfy thirsty. Wiggo, you're still up. Lead on."

Wiggins led them into the dark.

*

They stood at the top of a long flight of stone stairs heading down. Banks visualized the pyramid and the hill in his mind, and realized this staircase must run down the far outside of a structure built on the edge of the hill.

And somewhere down there, I bet there's a room, and a window, and our man.

All four of them wore the night goggles now, for there were no sconces on the walls here, no light source at all. Banks worried about the lack of resistance to their arrival. He expected to have met someone by now. But the corridor they descended into was narrow, and they had it covered front and rear. Any attack now was going to meet a rapid burst of fire from their rifles, enough to put anything short of an elephant down.

They descended fast, the steps taking them down in a steep, tight, spiral. They passed a window, little more than a slit in the rock at eye level, and heard the rush of water from outside again.

"We must be getting close," Banks said softly. "Keep it tight, lads. It's show time."

One more flight of steps brought them to a landing with three roughly hewed doors on the outward side. Banks motioned, and McCally put his shoulder, hard, into the nearest one. The door fell in with a crash, and a pale figure on the ground under the window yelled in sudden fear and crawled quickly into the corner with his hands up, protecting his head. Banks saw his face before it was covered. It wasn't Buller.

"We're here to help," McCally said, having to say it twice before the crouched, naked, man went quiet. The sudden lack of noise meant they could again hear the cascade outside, and the approach of running footsteps from somewhere above them.

"Wiggo, watch the stairs," Banks said, and moved quickly to the middle door. Without being asked, Hynd went to the third one at the other end of the corridor. Banks counted down from three on his finger, then they both took out their door. Banks found a dead man, again not Buller, in the middle room.

"Got him!" Hynd shouted. By the time Banks got out to the corridor, Hynd had emerged with another naked man, one who could barely stand on his own and was having to be half-carried out of the cell. When he looked up, Banks recognized his face from the video message. McCally came out of the first room, half-carrying the first man who looked too weak to stand on his own. Somewhere above them, the sound of running feet on stone was getting closer.

"Up or down, Cap?" Hynd said.

Going back up meant a firefight, but they knew the way out; down was too much of an unknown.

"Up," he said. "As fast as we can, and we go through anyone who gets in our way. Plugs in, lads. It's going to get noisy in here."

He addressed Hynd as all four of them shoved in the plastic plugs that protected their hearing from the worst of the impact of their shots.

"You and Cally bring these men as well as you can; Wiggo and I will plow the road."

They headed for the stairs and reached then in time to see the first attacker's lower body as he came down from above.

- 7 -

Wiggins stepped up first and raised his weapon. The man who came down at them either had no knowledge of rifles, or didn't care, for he came on fast with a long knife raised above his head. Wiggins didn't hesitate; he put two shots into the man's head, and stepped quickly up and over the body as it fell at his feet. Despite the plugs, the noise was almost deafening, and seemed to echo around them for long seconds. The dead man slumped all the way to the foot of the staircase. Banks had to step up quickly himself to avoid the sudden flow of blood on the steps.

"Watch your footing," he shouted back at the others, then went quickly after Wiggins who was already three steps up, and facing another attacker. This one was no more cautious than the first, although he was armed with a short spear that he stabbed toward Wiggins' face. Wiggins put him down the same way he'd done the first and was once again already on his way upstairs as the dead man fell.

Banks climbed up at Wiggins' back, weapon raised and ready to back the private up should help be needed. But the private was doing fine all on his own.

A third attacker went down as quickly as the first two, then all fell quiet above them; they climbed quickly up in almost dead silence except for the soft rush of tumbling water coming from out beyond the stairwell.

Banks noticed brighter light above. They were approaching

the top of the stairs. He tapped Wiggins on the shoulder and motioned that they should remove their goggles. They stood still for several seconds, letting their eyes adjust to the dim light, the flickering yellow and gold coming from the oil lanterns in the altar room above. Behind them, Hynd and McCally helped the two naked men hobble up the stairs. The man McCally was helping had to be almost lifted up every step, but he had a look of grim determination on his face that Banks took as a good sign. He waited until they were all in close formation before tapping Wiggins on the shoulder again.

"Last push, up and out and then off and clear to the boat," he whispered.

"Aye," Wiggins replied equally quietly. "This Indiana Jones shite is no' as much fun as it looks in the films."

They headed up the last six steps.

"Off and clear" was a forlorn hope.

*

The altar room at the top of the stairwell was packed tight with natives, a small forest of spears and long knives waiting in the doorway. Even then Banks might have chosen to shoot their way out, but a tall figure, his head covered in a scaled headdress shaped like a striking snake's head, stepped forward and poured fluid out of a large cauldron. The shimmer of oil rose in the air, and Banks tasted it, thick in his throat, even as it ran in a rivulet across the altar room floor and down the stairs at the squad's feet.

The tall figure took one of the oil lamp sconces from the wall and held it high while looking Banks directly in the eye. He didn't need to speak; the threat was clear enough. All he had to do was drop the lamp and the floor, the steps, and Banks' squad would instantly be engulfed in a raging wall of flame. It was not a death Banks chose for himself or for those in his charge.

"Cap?" Wiggins asked, looking for orders.

"Guns on the floor, lads, and step up and out. We can't win this here. Let's live to fight another day."

"Cap?" Wiggins said again. Banks knew that the private would prefer to go down swinging if he was going down.

"Stand down, Wiggo. That's an order. If not for me, then for these two poor bastards we rescued. Do you want to see them burn?"

When Banks stepped out into the altar room and dropped his gun, Wiggins was doing the same at his side.

*

"Just let us go and there won't be any trouble," Banks said, but the leader of the crowd gathered against them showed no sign of understanding. He motioned, a series of complicated hand signals, and three of them moved forward to quickly gather up the dropped rifles. Hynd and McCally were likewise quickly disarmed.

"You're getting yourself into big trouble here," Buller said behind Banks. "These men are soldiers. More will come. Let us go, and I won't press charges."

Wiggins laughed at that.

"I don't think these lads give a fuck about the Polis."

Things moved fast in the next few minutes. The squad and the two naked men were bundled back down the steps to the cells, their way lit only by flaming torches carried by their guards. The bodies they'd left behind on the way up were quickly dragged off into the dark, and although Banks tried to pick his way down carefully, he still felt the slide and slip of fresh blood under his soles as they descended.

Once on the landing, the armed men stripped the squad naked, their clothes, boots and goggles being spirited away back up the stairs. The leader found Banks' satellite phone and examined it, but not as if curious in any way as to its function, and only for a few seconds before it too was taken away.

Two of them threw Banks unceremoniously into the first cell. He landed hard and had to tumble in a well-practiced roll to avoid breaking a collarbone on the rough stone floor. Buller came in, stumbling behind him. He heard a ruckus outside, then Wiggins shouting loud curses before a thud—the distinctive sound of wood against skull—brought a sudden silence.

"Wiggo just tried something daft. He's down, but he's alive, Cap," Hynd shouted, then there was another short ruckus before silence fell again.

"Tell them to keep quiet," Buller said at his side. "They leave us alone if we're quiet. Mostly."

"Radio silence until my order," Banks shouted. No reply came back, but he didn't expect one. The door shut, and they heard a bar get put in place on the outside. Footsteps on stone echoed away up the stairwell, then they were left in the quiet dark.

*

Banks waited until he was sure they were completely alone, then made a quick survey of the cell in the dark with his fingers. It was little more than a 10-foot square block, solid stone everywhere including floor and even the ceiling, which he could just touch by standing on tiptoe. Opposite the doorway, he came to a tall window open to the elements that looked out over nothing but more darkness, only the shimmer and dance of the stars overhead showing any light. The only sound was the cascade of water, louder here, from somewhere over to his right.

"You threw the phone from here?" he asked. "I'm surprised it didn't just bounce off a rock and get bashed to buggery."

"It was a Hail Mary, that's for sure," Buller said. "But you obviously got the message. Where's the rest of the cavalry?"

"Next door," Banks said dryly.

Buller laughed.

"You four losers are the sum total of the fucking rescue team? And you just laid down your guns and let them throw you in here with me? Well, that's just fucking peachy."

"Aye, and I saved you from getting your bollocks roasted in the process. You're welcome," Banks replied. "Pleased to meet you too."

Buller didn't reply, but went to sit cross-legged on the floor in the corner. All Banks saw of him was a paler shape among the shadows. Banks walked back across the small cell to the door and tried his weight against it. It creaked, but held firm. He knew he could probably force it open by putting a shoulder to it, but that would attract attention, and they no longer had the advantage of firepower. He didn't fancy his chances naked and unarmed against a score or more men with knives and spears, no matter that he had the benefit of training.

"If I'd known you were going to be so fucking incompetent, I'd have asked for Gerald fucking Butler," Buller said from the darkness.

"Aye, well, if I'd known you were going to be such a gobby wee shite, I'd have let you fucking burn upstairs and we wouldn't be in this mess now."

"People don't talk to me like that."

"Why is that then? Because you're the son of a lord? In here, you're just another bollock-naked arsehole with the rest of us poor fuckers. So tell me what I need to know to get out of here, or shut the fuck up. Either way's fine by me."

Banks hoped he hadn't overdone it. If he read the man right, he'd get answers. Even if he had it wrong, it wouldn't be the first time he'd pissed off a peer of the realm, although he'd just earned himself a bollocking from the colonel if they ever got home.

It turned out he had indeed read the man right. Buller didn't move from his seated position, but when he spoke again it was softly, with more than a hint of fear in it.

"I need to tell you about the snakes."

*

"We're in the Amazon jungle. Of course there's going to be fucking snakes."

"Are you going to listen, or are you going to take the piss?"

I'm perfectly capable of both at the same time.

He didn't say it and bit his tongue. His man was still talking.

"I saw the first one at the same time I threw the phone out of the window," Buller continued. Banks didn't interrupt him. It wouldn't change anything to tell the man that they'd seen something too, and he needed the information.

"First it was a man, and then it wasn't," Buller said, his voice little more than a whisper in the dark.

"The guy in the full head mask? Aye, I saw him upstairs. We both did."

"No, he's their priest—more than that, he's some kind of shaman. But he's a man, and real enough. I meant the ones who can turn. If the superstitions are right, they call themselves the Children of Boitata."

"Now that name I have heard. It's some local snake god, isn't it?"

"And it's more than superstition," Buller whispered. "I've seen the Children change, man into snake into man again like something out of a film. But a film has never made me piss myself."

"Stop havering, man," Banks said, "and tell me something concrete I can use here."

"I'm telling you what I know, what I've seen," the sitting man said. "We're in uncharted country here, and it belongs to the snakes."

"Snakes or no snakes, my job is to get you home to your rich daddy, so tighten your sphincter man. I need you focused."

"You don't understand," Buller said. "There's no fucking point in being focused. We're next."

"Next for what?"

"You saw it upstairs," Buller said. "You must have had a good look at the altar on the way in. They cut Jack Baillie open, and they made me watch."

"Made you watch the cutting?"

"No," Buller said, almost shouting. "I told you, you don t understand. They cut him open. He was still alive, at least for long enough to watch as they dragged the guts out of him. Then they ripped out his heart. Then the snakes came, and they fed."

His voice dropped to a sob as he repeated what he'd said a minute before.

"We're next."

- 8 -

Buller's sobbing told Banks that the conversation was over, for now. That was probably for the best, for Banks could make little sense of what the man had been trying to explain. All Banks knew was that somewhere down the line he'd miscalculated the situation, and lost control of it. It was time to take it back, or at least make a start in that direction.

First up was to get their kit back from wherever it had been taken. The only way to do that was to get out of the cell quietly. And there was only the one exit that wasn't being watched.

He stepped quickly over to the window and leaned out. The wall was vertical both above and below, and stretched away on either side. He had a fair idea of how far they had descended from the top, but had no idea how far the structure might extend, or how far it was down to the canopy or river far below. He heard the cascade again, louder now. When he leaned out farther he felt spray, wet on his cheeks. That was going to make any attempt at a climb even trickier. He ran his hands over the stone where he could reach it. It was rough and eroded; plenty of finger and toeholds, but wet meant slippery.

Buller spoke softly.

"There's no way out that way. It's a 200-foot vertical drop," he said.

"Thank fuck for that," Banks replied. "I thought for a minute it was going to be fucking dangerous."

"You can't seriously be considering going out there?"

"Not considering, no. I've already made my mind up. If anybody comes looking for me, tell them I snapped and jumped."

Without waiting for a reply, he stepped up onto the window ledge, turned to face inward, then reached for a handhold he hoped was there. His fingers found what his eyes couldn't see, and he gripped, stepped, and reached with his other hand with the easy movements of a practiced climber.

The only way to do this was to act as if it was little more than a practice exercise. He visualized it as a wall in a gymnasium, where the only fall would be a short, non-fatal one, for to think of anything else would lead to doubt, and that would be a killer on such an ascent.

He'd climbed solo and unfettered before, free ascents of rock faces in the Cairngorms and Snowdonia, but this was a first—naked and already damp with spray from the cascade off to his left. His toes went in the place his fingers had been, his right hand went up, searched, found another hold, and pulled. He was getting into the rhythm of it now, allowing himself to lean away and not hug the wall, trusting his muscle memory and strength to keep him on the move upward. He considered dropping down to one of the other windows, to alert the others to his plan, but changing direction now would be risky; so upward it would be, fast enough to keep ahead of the worry.

His eyes had adjusted to the night completely now. The rock in front of him glistened where the stars danced in the fine drops of spray. Off to his right, the shimmering snake of the river seemed to writhe and squirm and now that he was higher he saw, to his left, the long silver cascade of a thin waterfall, some 30 yards away, tumbling noisily down into the darkness.

He reached for another grip as the sky blazed orange and red and the soft hiss, then thump, of an exploding flare lit up the wall in a blinding flash. For a bad second, he thought he might slip, but his toehold held, and he was able to reach and pull, and regain his momentum as gunshots rang out loud from somewhere far below him. Giraldo and Wilkes were in trouble, but there was nothing he could do to help them and seconds later, the flare had fallen away into darkness and the night fell silent again. He could only hope that the guide had managed to affect an escape.

He turned his attention back to the climb.

*

He moved as quickly as he could allow himself to without taking undue risks. His arms felt the strain now, the ache settling in his muscles, but he refused to acknowledge that, or the pain from flayed skin on fingers and toes. His knuckles also bled, from where he'd had to ram his fist into one particular hold to take his weight as he scrambled. But more than anything else, he felt alive, and realized he was grinning widely even as he hauled himself inch by inch up the wet wall.

He lost track of time. There was only the rhythm of hand and toehold, the wall and the movement. He was surprised to finally reach up and find not a hold, but a ledge. He hauled himself up onto the very top of the structure, on the roof of the cube that sat on top of what he'd thought to be a pyramid, but was obviously only stepped on the other three sides. The wall he had climbed fell away sheer below him, and now that he had the benefit of the height, he saw that it was a single face, all the way down to where it butted against the canopy far below.

He noted too that he was now above the source of the torrent, which was below him to his right where he stood on the ledge. The rush of water was still the only sound in the clear night air. Looking over the edge, he could only see the darkness of the jungle, and the silver of the shimmering snake of the river. He turned and made his way across the roof of the altar room, creeping slowly forward to get a view over the village, hoping that all would be quiet and that he might get a chance to search for their kit.

That hope was dashed almost immediately. He had got far enough across the roof to see down the length of the main causeway along the ridge of the hill and saw, at the far end, the flicker of approaching firebrands. He got down on his belly, feeling cold wet stone along the length of his body, and kept low. He shuffled as far back as he could while maintaining a line of sight, and could only watch as a crowd of 20 came toward the pyramid. Banks' heart sank when he saw that they had Wilkes with them, the big man being half-pushed, half-carried in a stumbling, limping walk.

*

Banks looked through the approaching crowd in vain for their guide, but there was no sign of Giraldo. Yet again he could only hope that the man had, somehow, made an escape. But for now, he only had eyes for Wilkes. There had obviously been a fight. The man bled from his nose, and a scalp wound above his left eye that had left the whole of that side of his shirt wet and red. There was also something wrong with his right leg, giving him a pronounced limp that was almost a slump, forcing his captors to push and shove him roughly to keep him in a straight line.

Banks checked for weapons. The villagers carried more of the long knives and spears he had seen earlier but there was no sign of the squad's rifles, or Wilkes' handgun. Banks hoped that it was the case that the villagers had no concept of modern weaponry and had simply discarded the guns, and that the kit would be stashed somewhere in the structure below him. But there was no way to get at it immediately. The small procession was already making its way up the pyramid steps, with Wilkes being poked and prodded ever more roughly as he faltered on the climb.

Banks stayed hidden. He was naked, weaponless, and any attempt at heroic rescue would only lead to a quick death under the knives and spears. He had to crawl backward as the oncoming crowd approached to avoid giving away his position, and wasn't far enough forward to see anything once they pushed Wilkes ahead of them into the cubic room below.

He didn't have to see to have a good idea what was going on. The screams started almost immediately and having already seen a body on the altar earlier, Banks could see all too clearly in his minds' eye the atrocities that were now being inflicted on the big man. Once again, he had almost overwhelming urge to intervene, to leap down and throw himself into the fray. But he'd been trained better than that, well enough for sense to override instinct, and he lay there, still and quiet as Wilkes' screams turned to frantic, animalistic howling that was, thankfully, not long lived.

Another noise replaced the screams, a slithering, moist, wetness that Banks thought must be what remained of Wilkes being hollowed out like the earlier man. Then he smelled it, an acrid odor in the air, like hot oil and vinegar. It was accompanied by more slithering, louder now, a sound that so perplexed Banks that he had to crawl forward several inches to sate his curiosity.

He looked down to the entrance of the room below him in time to see the first of them emerge. It was a snake, a huge, rainbow-hued thing some fifteen feet in length, and as thick as a man's thigh at its thickest point. It slid down the pyramid steps and away into the night while Banks was still trying to process what he'd seen. There was no hope of considering it a hallucination. In short order, another, then another, then more of the massive snakes slid and slithered out of the room below, off down the steps and scattered into the shadows in the ruins.

He counted 20 of them.

- 9 -

Banks waited. He kept an eye on the steps and the shadows in the ruins, but the snakes had effectively disappeared. The only sound was the soft tumble of water from the cascade off to the side of the pyramid, and the only light showing was the yellow-gold flicker from the lamps that still burned in the chamber below him. He lay there feeling sweat cool on his body, noticing that the acrid oily odor was fading fast. After 10 minutes, he felt safe enough to creep to the lip of the roof. He lowered himself down to the top step of the pyramid to one side of the doorway so that he wouldn't frame himself in the light from inside. He kept a close eye on the shadowed ruins below, ready to flee at the first hint of snake activity, and sidled sideward, backing into the altar room.

He'd already known he'd see it, but the sight of poor Wilkes splayed out, still wet, on the altar, dead eyes staring accusingly, shook Banks to the core. He averted his gaze and made a quick circuit of the room, looking for their kit and weapons. All he found was clothing and blades discarded in random piles on the floor by the natives.

Snakes have no need for clothes. Snakes have no hands to carry a knife in.

He laughed, then caught himself before any sound escaped. A manic madness fluttered in his head, a need to be off and away from this place where nothing made much of any sense.

He turned for one more look at the body on the altar, trying not to think about the blood trails that led off and away down the pyramid steps. Poor Wilkes was beyond any help.

But the squad needs me.

That single thought was enough to get him moving. He put on a kilt-like piece of cloth that he was able to tie at his waist, and although it barely covered the essentials, he felt somehow less vulnerable for wearing it. Another look round confirmed that their kit was nowhere in the room, so he gathered up as much loose clothing, and as many blades, as he could safely carry into a bundle under his left arm. With his free hand, he carefully took down one of the oil lamps and carried it ahead of him as he headed for the stairs.

*

Buller was still sitting cross-legged on the floor and looked up in astonishment when Banks entered the cell two minutes later.

"Are you ready to be rescued yet or are you still to feert to move?" Banks asked. Buller got, somewhat unsteadily, to his feet.

"I thought for sure you'd fallen. You've been gone for hours."

Banks passed him a loincloth and left him to figure out how to put it on while he went and opened the other two doors. Hynd, McCally, and Wiggins were all up and awake. Wiggins had an egg-shaped bruise at his left temple, but seemed little the worse for the bump on the head earlier. Banks passed them each a cloth.

The other man they'd found earlier was slumped against a wall in the third cell, and McCally stopped Banks from stepping over to him.

"He died a couple of hours back, Cap," the corporal said. "Went in his sleep with no pain, which I think must have been a blessing for him. Dehydration or starvation, it's hard to tell what got him first. He was delirious for a wee bit before sleep got him.

Some shite about snakes or something."

Banks turned to Buller.

"Was he one of yours?"

The man didn't seem particularly moved at the death.

"Aye. Poor bastard. He was taken a few days before me. Can we go?"

"I'm touched by your fucking concern," McCally said.

Buller laughed bitterly.

"He got paid well enough."

Banks held McCally back. For a moment, it looked like the corporal might hit the man. Wiggins took a long knife from the pile Banks had dropped on the floor.

"Here I was thinking this was an Indiana Jones story, but look at me now... I'm bloody Tarzan."

"Nah," Hynd said, taking a knife for himself. "I'm Tarzan. You're the fucking chimpanzee."

"Can it, lads," Banks said, and turned to Buller who was still at the door of the cell where the dead man lay.

"I'm not keen on going back up top from here," he said. "Can we go down the other way?"

Buller shrugged.

"I've not been that way. Your guess is as good as mine," he said.

Hynd motioned at the knives and spears they were carrying.

"No sign of our gear, Cap?"

"Nope. And no time to go hunting around in the dark for it either. If we make it back to the dredger, there's all the gear we left there, so that's our priority. I've had enough of this place. We go down; if all else fails, at least we'll have a shorter jump into the river."

He passed the oil lamp to Buller.

"You stay in the middle of the group. And whatever the fuck you do, don't drop this. I've done enough fucking about in the dark already tonight."

"What's the plan, Cap?" Hynd asked as Banks led them toward the downward steps.

"Get away clean, back to the dredger, and call for an evac so we can get rid of this arsehole here. That middle part might be a problem, depending on whether Giraldo's still around or not."

"And Wilkes," Hynd replied, then went quiet when he saw the look on Banks' face.

"Wilkes?" Buller said. "You didn't bring that daft sod with you, did you?"

Banks kept walking and didn't reply. The last thing that was needed now was any explanation of the carnage he'd seen upstairs, even if he felt like doing it if only to see if he could get any emotion at all out of the man they'd come to save.

He stepped to the top of the stairs, Hynd at his side, with Buller in the middle carrying the flickering oil lamp, and Wiggins and McCally bringing up the rear.

*

The oil lamp only gave out enough light to see a few yards ahead at a time, and even then both Hynd's and Banks' shadows loomed large in the dark, obscuring much of the view. Banks considered taking the lamp himself, but he needed his hands free in case it came to a sudden fight. They took the descent as fast as was practical under the circumstances.

The walls here were still worked stone, but their placement and build showed a more ancient origin even than the pyramid and altar room above. Age had eroded both the walls and the steps at their feet, the rock being cold and worn smooth underfoot. Banks wondered how many long ages that men—and other things—had been traveling up and down these same steps.

It was a steep descent, and a twisting one. Every so often,

they'd pass another of the small-slit windows and hear the distant rush of the cascade. But apart from the fall of water, the only other sound was their own feet on the stone and the occasional spit and splutter from the oil lamp. The air got more damp and clammy the farther down they went, and after a time the stone ran wet, and it got slippery underfoot, so that they had to slow to avoid tumbling away into the dark.

"We're running out of oil," Buller whispered from behind Hynd.

"It can't be too much farther now," Banks said. He'd been counting steps, and trying to gauge distance from what he remembered of the drop from the nighttime climb.

We must be getting close, at least to the level of the canopy.

But still there were no windows accessible enough to give them a view as to their position, and they kept going down, following their own shifting shadows into the dark well below.

Then he smelled it, acrid, hot oil and vinegar. Somewhere below—and not too far below—something heavy moved, a darker shadow in the blackness. Banks knew that if they were caught in an open area by the mass of the snake things he'd seen on the pyramid steps, they'd be either caught again or, more likely, slaughtered within seconds. But having come this far, he was in no mood for retreat.

"Come on then, let's see what you've got, you wanker," he said and stepped forward with his knife held in front of him.

- 10 -

He'd only taken two steps when he realized Buller wasn't following and that he had stepped down into the darkest of the shadows. By then it was too late, and his blood was up in any case. He yelled, a formless cry of frustration and rage, and swung the knife, fast, toward where he thought he'd seen movement. He was rewarded with hitting something solid, feeling the blade cut, and hot liquid splashing on his hand, bringing with it a far stronger, more acrid odor that stung at the back of his throat and caused his eyes to water. He fought off the urge to retreat and went one more step down, stabbing the knife ahead of him again and again, hitting soft warm flesh with every second or third thrust. Then he was merely stabbing at air, and he sensed rather than saw something huge and serpentine move away downward at speed. The air cleared somewhat, and the stench became at least bearable.

"Buller! Get that fucking light down here. I want to see what we're facing."

But when he turned to shout, he saw something else. He could see the men on the stairs above him, silhouetted where thin light penetrated through a window slit, and it was already getting brighter.

They'd seen out the night.

Dawn was coming.

*

He stood, waiting for the men to come down to him, looking down into the stairwell below him. It was now light enough to see the steps at his feet. They were coated with slimy fluid.

"Fucking hell, Cap," Hynd said. "What have you got on your hand? It's bloody minging."

Banks looked at the knife, which dripped with the gray-green slime. The fluid coated his hand up to the wrist and over some of his forearm. It was sticky to the touch, and gave off the now recognizable acrid odor.

"Snake shite, at a guess," he said and wiped blade and hand on the scrap of material serving as his kilt. As he looked down, he saw the slime on the steps at his feet, glistening, almost glowing, in the gloom, a trail leading away downward.

"I've wounded it, whatever the fuck it was. It came in from somewhere, and it'll be going out somewhere. Come on, lads, let's get the flock out of here. Mind your feet, the sarge is right—this stuff's fucking worse than dog shite on Sauchihall Street."

He turned again to Buller.

"And the next time I move in the dark, you fucking move with me, or I'll leave you here. Got it?"

Buller tried to look Banks in the eye, but his gaze slid away, and the lamp trembled in his hand, causing the flame to flicker. When the man took a step down toward Banks and Hynd, the flame wavered.

"It wasn't me," Buller wailed, but Banks shushed him.

"There's a draft here. Quickly now, follow me."

Once again, he led them down. This time, they weren't quite descending into darkness; thin sunlight filtered in through all the window-slits, and the green slime at their feet glistened, as if catching the rays and reflecting them back. Within a dozen steps, the passageway opened out into a wider, circular chamber. On the far side from where they stood, an open archway showed sunlight, streaming in from outside and falling across a naked body lying on the floor.

At some point in the trail from stairwell to doorway, the green slime turned red. When Banks walked over, and turned the body face up, it was a dead man's face that looked up at him, a man who had bled out from deep knife wounds to chest and abdomen.

"What the fuck is this now?" Hynd said softly, looking down at the slime trail, then at the body.

"I'll try to explain if we get time," Banks replied. "But if you see any snakes, big or small, stab them first and ask questions later."

He looked around for Buller. The man was over on the far side of the rocky chamber from the doorway, with the lamp lifted up toward the roughly hewn rock of the roof where it met the wall above his head.

"Time to go," Banks said.

Buller didn't reply at first, merely held the lamp higher above his head. When he did finally speak, it was in a whisper of awe. He pointed to a shinier patch of the wall above, a patch that glistened, more yellow, more golden, than the light from the lamp. It ran, in a vein as thick as a tree trunk, one with a huge network of branches, all across the roof of the chamber.

"Go? We can't go, not now that we've found this. Do you know what this is?"

"It's a distraction, that's what it is. Now come on. We're getting the fuck out of here, and we're doing it right now."

"You don't understand," Buller said. "This is a seam. It's gold. It's fucking millions of pounds worth of gold and probably the mother lode of everything we get from the river. We've only gone and found the bloody source."

"Aye, very nice," Banks replied. "But it'll be no bloody use to man nor beast if you get eaten by a big fucking snake. Now move your arse, or we'll go without you."

That was an idle threat, and they both knew it, but Buller finally saw sense, and moved away toward the doorway. When they reached the body, Banks took the lamp. There was only a dribble of oil left in it. He tipped the lamp until the flame ran over the fuel then poured the oil, flaming as it fell, into the dead man's mouth.

"Just in case," he said.

Thick black smoke rose from the gullet. Banks waited long enough to ensure the body wasn't about to slither to life, then he turned and walked quickly to the open archway to avoid the smell of burning flesh.

*

The archway led out onto a rocky track that ran along the base of the structure they had exited. Looking up, Banks saw the vertical tower looming high over them. Going left, the path headed in an upward slope, back up toward the high ridge of the hillside above them. Going right, it led gently downward toward the cascading torrent that could now be clearly seen and heard some 30 yards away.

Banks considered back going up to the pyramid complex. Now that it was daylight, they might have a chance of finding and recovering their kit and more importantly, weaponry. But Buller was the priority here, and now they had their man out of captivity so close to the river, it would be folly to put him back in harm's way so soon. He didn't hesitate and took the downward path, hoping to reach the riverside quay, and hoping against hope that Giraldo had somehow evaded the attention of the natives when Wilkes had been taken. If not, and both their guide and boat were gone, they were in for a long walk—and swim—back down river to the dredger, and he didn't want to think of how long that might take them.

First things first, and one step at a time.

He headed down the slope toward the cascade, and the squad, with Wiggins pushing Buller along none too gently, followed at his back.

*

Spray from the waterfall coated the track, making the rock underfoot slippery. When Banks licked his lips, he noted how fresh and cool the water was, and realized how dry his throat and mouth had become.

I've been neglecting the basics.

He stepped forward to where a small stream ran between the stones and cupped his hands to take a drink.

When he stood back, he felt better than he had for a while, and reminded himself to keep a closer eye on their water intake; dehydration would kill them as fast as anything else in this heat.

"Drink up, lads. We're going to need to keep hydrated. And we might not get too many chances."

He watched the track while the others drank. The sun beat hard from a clear sky. Heat rose from the rocks in waves. The day was warming up fast.

"Keep moving," he said. "Fast as you can, lads. There'll at least be shade under the canopy and down at the riverside."

"How about a pub, Cap?" Wiggins said. "I could murder a pint of lager."

"You and me both, lad," Banks replied. "But if it'll get you to move your arse, remember, there's beer in the fridge back on the dredger. If we all get back there in one piece, the first round is on me."

The banter, even if somewhat forced, seemed to perk the squad up, and they moved out as a unit, with Buller sandwiched in the middle, heading under a rocky overhang that took them beneath the cascade itself, into a narrow natural cave. The roar of the water was almost deafening here, but it was cooler, and Banks let the squad stand in the fresher air for a minute before moving them out and down again. The combined effects of drinking the colder water and standing here in the shade cleared Banks' head of a fog the heat had been bringing on, and he was moving faster and with more purpose when he led them back out onto the downward side of the trail.

The track continued to wind downward. They were now well below the base of the tower, with bare, unworked rock butting up close to the track on their right and a sheer drop of 30 feet or more to their left. When Banks looked over, he saw they were closing on the top area of forest canopy, and several minutes later they had descended into the dense, lush, vegetation of the forest. Almost immediately the humidity level rose and it felt like walking in a sauna. The insect population took note of them again, and this time nobody had any cigarettes with which to dispel the biting swarms. They ploughed downhill as fast as they could manage, looking for escape, or even respite.

The trail narrowed, then narrowed again, the green of the jungle encroaching on both sides as they descended away from the rocky hill toward the river. Soon Banks, in the lead, had to resort to hacking and slashing with the heavy knife to clear the way ahead. The only solace he drew was that it looked like they were the first to have come this way for quite some time.

*

It proved to be hard going under the humidity and after a few minutes, he had to step back and let Hynd take the lead with the hacking.

"Do you know what the fuck you're doing?" Buller asked.

Banks resisted another almost overwhelming urge to punch the man out, and answered calmly.

"Saving your arse," he said and turned his back before the temptation got too great to ignore.

"It's getting thinner ahead, Cap," Hynd said. "I think we're nearly through."

He motioned Banks forward for a look. They had arrived at the river and were about to emerge at one end of the stone quay they'd left the night before. The docking area beneath the run of steps sat quiet and empty; their boat and guide was nowhere to be seen.

- 11 -

"Now what?" Buller said, too loudly, at Banks' back.

"Now we're royally fucked," Hynd said.

"Can't you build a raft or something?"

"Aye," Wiggins replied from the rear. "Maybe we could at that. But it would be easier to hollow you out and use you as a fucking canoe."

Banks had a sudden memory, a flash of Wilkes on the altar, scraped clean on the inside. He felt gorge rise in his throat as he turned and hushed the others with a finger to his lips.

"Stow it, Wiggo," he said in little more than a whisper. "Behave yourself if you want that beer."

He turned back and, motioning for Hynd to come with him, stepped out of the foliage onto the quay. The stone underfoot was baking hot, even this early in the day, and Banks kept moving, aware that to stand still might raise blisters on the soles of his feet in no time. They walked the length of the dock and partly along the hillside track they'd taken the night before, looking for any clue as to what might have happened. They found two shell casings, from Wilkes' gun he guessed, and a smear of blood that led them to a trail of spatter that in turn led farther off along the stone pathway back up to the hill.

"This is where they got Wilkes," he said to Hynd.

"Aye, I guess so," Hynd said. "I saw the flare and heard the shots in the night. Any clue as to what went down?"

"No, but I know what happened to the big man."

They were out of hearing range of the others now, so Banks gave his sergeant a quick rundown of what he'd seen from atop the pyramid during the night and the snakes' feeding ceremony.

"Fucking hell, Cap," Hynd said. "What are we into this time? And where the fuck's our boat?"

"The answer to both is the same, Sarge. I don't have a Scooby. But we're running out of options. I'm thinking I'd rather use a raft than take a swim."

"I'm with you on that, Cap," Hynd replied. "But will we get the time to build it? Are those big snakes round do you think? And can they swim?"

Banks shrugged.

"I don't have any answers for you, Sarge, and I don't really care. We're getting out of here, one way or another. And I'm with Wiggo. I could murder one of those beers back in the dredger. Come on, let's get started. I want us back on that rig before it gets dark again. I've got a feeling we'll need to be tooled up for whatever else is coming."

*

They spent the next hours alternately seeking shade and water and taking turns in chopping vines and assessing what tree branches might be of best use in the building of what would have to be a rough and ready raft. McCally found some large nuts that, when cracked open, proved to be edible when washed down with water and took the edge off what was a growing hunger.

While the work proceeded, Buller sat in a shaded spot on the edge of the quay, and refused point blank to help in any way.

"I'm the fucking job, aren't I?" he said. "Just fucking rescue me, will you? Once we get that gold out of that rock, I'll make you all rich men."

68

Wiggins looked up at Banks from where he was trying to lash three poles together with a braided rope made of stripped bark.

"I still like my idea of using him as a canoe," he said.

"Best idea you've had in years, Wiggo," Banks replied. "But the lad's father is a big shot back home and wants him back. Although I'm fucked if I can see why."

He spoke loud enough to ensure that Buller heard, and waited to see if there would be a comeback, but the man stayed seated, staring out at the river. Banks went back to helping Wiggins lash poles together.

*

By the time they were nearly ready to get their raft into the water, the sun had already passed its highest point overhead, but they'd been allowed to go about the build without anything attacking them. It seemed that, if their escape had been noted, nobody was all that bothered about finding them. But that thought only got Banks thinking about snakes again, and to wondering how long it might be before they returned to human form, to themselves.

He didn't want anything more to do with Buller than he had to, but he had questions, and the man might have answers. He left the others to get the raft in the water and test it out for strength and buoyancy, and went to talk to the man they were tasked with rescuing.

"Where are they?" he said, without preamble.

"They mostly come out at night," Buller said, not looking around. "I think they don't like the sun."

"Then we're safe?"

Buller laughed bitterly.

"That's not the word I'd use. But we're as safe as we're going to be as long as we stay out here in the open. But I'm not a fucking expert, you know?"

Oh, I know that just fine.

He didn't say it, and didn't push for more information, for by that time the others had the raft floating below them, with Wiggins using a large paddle as a rudder. McCally and Hynd were using two smaller, spade-like paddles to propel the structure, somewhat unsteadily, along the side of the quay.

Banks got Buller to his feet and the two of them stepped gingerly aboard. The raft wasn't that much larger than a wide door, and it rocked alarmingly, then steadied under their weight.

"Careful, Cap," Wiggins said from the back. "She goes well enough in a straight line, but she's a bit too chunky for anything complicated. A bit like the sarge's wife."

Buller sat squarely in the middle, cross-legged, and already looking off into space. Banks ignored the man and knelt at the front where he could give direction, and warn them of anything ahead in the water.

The quay sat in a sheltered inlet, and they managed to navigate easily enough in the relatively still waters on their way out to the river itself. Banks looked up, to the wall that towered high above to his left, and picked out his climbing route of the night before, now marveling that he'd managed it without falling and getting dashed on the rocky hill below. He was also looking out for any attack, for now would be a good time for one, if their opponents had any tactical savvy. But no arrows, rocks, or spears came down from higher up, and they emerged out into the Amazon, where the current hit them side on and immediately threatened to tumble them away at its mercy.

The first few minutes were a frantic flurry of paddling and rearranging their weight while Banks tried to gauge the river ahead and shout out a course of least resistance to the flow. Several times they nearly tumbled over completely and river water washed over the top of the raft, threatening to sink them. But eventually

Wiggins got the hang of the makeshift rudder, and McCally and Hynd were able to work in tandem to stabilize the raft and get it moving with rather than against the flow. By the time they got going in a straight line, they were 30 yards and more from the right-hand bank, heading down river almost sedately.

Banks had a last look back at the high tower where they'd been held. It already looked much smaller, almost insignificant when measured against the magnificence of the wide snaking river. Then all his attention was on the water itself, as he watched for eddies or cross currents that might throw them off course.

- 12 -

The squad seemed to have the hang of controlling the raft, and they made good time with the help of the current, but now the main thing worrying Banks wasn't the river itself, but the baking sun above them, and their complete lack of protection from it. They had hours on the water ahead of them yet, and he already felt a vise-like grip around his skull, and a tightening of the skin across his shoulders. Heatstroke, and crippling sunburn, was an all too real threat.

The left bank of the river was in shadow and would stay that way now for the afternoon and evening to come, but that was 100 yards away across the strongest of the current—there was no certainty they could make it across without being toppled. When he saw a large inlet on the right side bank ahead, with a heavy overhang of canopy, he didn't hesitate.

"Hang a right, Wiggo," he shouted. "Over to the bank. Let's get out of the sun and wait it out for a bit."

Buller looked up at that, and for the first time Banks saw a worried look on the man's face.

"It'll be dark again before you know it," he said. "We haven't come far enough yet."

"We'll fry if we try to go any farther in this," he replied.

"It might be worth the risk," Buller said, but still wouldn't look Banks in the eye. And although Buller was the mission, the squad needed to be strong and fit enough to see it through.

And for that, we need to find shade. Right now.

Wiggins didn't hesitate, and steered them, hard and fast, toward the bank. Helped by a cross current at the mouth of the inlet, they got pushed inside, only to come up hard against the keel of a boat that was already berthed there.

As luck would have it, they had found their guide.

*

Giraldo was in no state to welcome them. When they clambered up into the boat, they found the guide in a cot under the makeshift tent that covered the rear end of the vessel. The man lay, staring into space, eyes wide open. At first, Banks thought he was dead and gone, but as he got closer, he saw the sweat at the man's brow, and the slow, too slow, rise and fall of his chest as he breathed.

"Giraldo?" Banks said, bending over the man. The guide's eyes flickered, and, painfully slowly, he turned his head. He had tears, whether of pain or sorrow Banks could not tell, in his eyes when he spoke.

"I could not save Mr. Wilkes," he whispered. "Then I waited, but you did not come. And I waited too long to do anything about this."

He raised an arm, and Banks saw the two black holes three inches apart in the man's upper arm. The skin around the wounds was already gray and necrotic.

"I am sorely bit, Captain," the guide said and, as if that had used all his strength, he slumped back onto the cot, staring at the canvas above him.

"Wiggo, Cally, get us out of here. We need to get this man a doctor, right now."

Buller spoke at his side.

"It's too late for him," the man said, with about as much

emotion as if he was commenting on the weather. "I've seen the like before. He'll be gone by nightfall."

"Aye? Is that so?" Banks replied. "Well, maybe not. We can call in aerial support from the dredger. And if not, I'd prefer it if you shut the fuck up and let the man die in peace."

"People don't talk to me like that."

"Aye, you've told me that already. And I just did, again. If you don't like it, you can always fuck off for a swim."

Despite the heat, Buller went to sit up the front of the boat, out from under the shade of the tent.

"If the wanker wants to fry, that's fine by me," Hynd said at Banks' back.

"And me, Sarge," Banks said, and bent again to check on Giraldo, but the guide had said what he needed to say, and had gone back to concentrating on staying alive.

"Hang in there, man," Banks said. "We'll get you home."

Wiggins got the engine running at the first attempt, and minutes later they were out of the inlet and back on the river, pushing along as fast as they could manage, heading for the dredger.

*

McCally raided the boat's stores, which were in a long box under the driver's seat, and got a pot of coffee brewing on a tiny camp stove while he handed out some tough, dried fish. He held up a battered, almost full, pack of the black cigarettes.

"And I found his stash," he said, gleefully. "Who needs a fag?"

Banks took control of the wheel. The rest of the squad smoked, drank coffee, and chewed fish jerky and all in all, Banks was starting to feel a lot better about life in general; they'd got their man, although he was indeed a wanker, and they were managing to beat a retreat in some comfort. All that was needed now was to get to the dredger, secure the place, and call in somebody to evacuate them post-haste.

The only source of worry for him was the fate of their guide.

"Wiggo?" The private looked up. "Spell me for a couple of minutes. I want to check on your pal on the cot."

"Remind him he promised to get me tickets to Brazil's next match, so he'd better not fucking die on me."

Banks went to check on Giraldo, leaving Wiggins at the wheel. The bit man still stared, unseeing, at the tent above him. The gray skin around the bites had spread, tendrils, almost black, snaking up and around his upper arm toward his shoulder. His temperature was up, and heat came off him in waves, accompanied by an acrid odor and vinegary tang that was far too close to the snake smells Banks had encountered earlier.

"Can we get any more speed out of this jalopy?" he asked Wiggins.

"Not from the engine, Cap," the private said. "But we can head farther out into the river and try to catch the main current? That would get the speed up."

"Make it so," Banks said. He brushed a pair of black flies from in front of his nose, but others replaced them almost immediately. He gave in to the inevitable and helped himself to one of the cigarettes. Now seemed as good a time as any to return to bad habits.

*

Wiggins was as good as his word, and found the fast current in the center of the river, after which they made much quicker progress. After 10 minutes or so, Buller realized the futility of sulking up front in the baking sun and moved to join the rest under the canopy of canvas, although he still would not look any of them in the eye.

Banks chewed on a second smoke as he sipped at the too strong, too bitter coffee McCally had brewed up. The cigarettes were unfiltered, and rough but strangely familiar to Banks, reminding his of the smell and taste of the full-tar, full-strength ones his granddad had smoked in the greenhouse while Banks helped with the growing of his tomatoes in the summers of childhood. The heat here was more brutal than those long ago days in Scotland, but he held tight to the memory, a guide to see him on his way home from this river.

He'd had enough of the coffee though. He poured the dregs from the tin cup over the side, and was about to flick the butt of the cigarette away when a hot hand gripped his wrist. He looked to his left, to see Giraldo trying to push himself off the cot.

Banks moved quickly to force the man back down, then fetched some water, which the guide swallowed down in two huge gulps.

"Smoke," Giraldo said. Banks felt obliged to refuse, but the guide was insistent, so he lit another, and passed it over, placing it gently between the man's lips.

"Obrigado," the guide said quietly and sucked in a prodigious draw that would have had Banks choking.

"Try to rest," Banks said. "I reckon we'll be back at the dredger in a couple of hours, then we'll get a chopper to lift you out."

"You are a good man, Captain," the guide said. "It is a pity your effort will be in vain. The black venom leaves no survivors—we all know that here on the river. I will go with the sun."

"Don't talk pish, man. Besides, you can't go yet. Wiggo's got a date at the next Brazil game, and you said you had a story to tell me."

Giraldo laughed, then coughed so hard Banks thought he might expire on the spot, before recovering and smiling thinly.

"Ask Private Wiggins to take my boy to the match. And as for the story, I had best tell you," he said. "For it is a tale you ought to know. But first, I must speak more of last night."

"You don't need to speak at all…" Banks started, but Giraldo stopped him.

"But I do. Mr. Wilkes deserves it from me, for I see he is not here, and that only means one thing. The Children of Boitata took him."

It wasn't a question, and Banks did not need to answer. He sat beside the man, passing him frequent sips of water, and let him speak.

- 13 -

"Mr. Wilkes was most fretful, almost immediately after you and your men walked into the jungle," he began. "Several times I had to dissuade him from stomping off after you, and even almost half a bottle of my rum did not settle him—indeed, I believe it made things worse. Emboldened by the drink, he started to berate me, you, the company he worked for, everybody under the sun. Then he loudly proclaimed that he would 'sort this shit out once and for all' and before I could stop him, he took out his pistol and jumped up onto the quay. He ran off onto the trail before I even got off the boat. I knew it was madness to try and follow him, and I thought to warn you. I readied a flare, and fired. It had only just gone up, lighting the sky, when I heard shooting. Then, before I could give any thought to going to Mr. Wilkes' aid, it came for me, out of the jungle, one of Boitata's children, slithering so fast I did not see it until it was on me.

"I want you to know, my friend, that my first thought was of you, and your safety. I was glad that I had fired the flare. Although it alerted the snake to my presence and cost me this bite that will soon take me to the dark, I regret nothing. Although I did not wait there in the dark for you, you are here now, and safe, and I can go to the darkness with my honor intact."

The effort of talking had taken what little strength the man had left, and he slumped down on the cot, his eyes sunk in deep black shadows. Banks saw that the black tracery of venom was now creeping toward his neck and across his chest. It would be all over when it reached his heart or his brain; it was only a matter of which went first.

"You did more than any man should be asked to do," Banks said. "I owe you a debt, so you had better stay with us, for I intend to pay it."

Giraldo tried to laugh, but all that come out was a dry rasp that turned into a coughing fit. Banks held the man's head up while he gave him more water. The guide's skin felt like a hot skillet, and there were flecks of black at his lips when Banks took the cup of water away.

"Thank you, my friend," the man said. "If you really wish to repay a debt, then I have only one last thing to tell you. Listen to my tale. Perhaps there is something in it that will save you and your men from meeting the darkness yourselves."

*

Banks thought the man was too spent for further talk, but Giraldo seemed determined, although Banks had to lean close to hear, for the guide's voice was close to failing completely now.

"I have been on this river every day of my life," he said, "but I only ever saw Boitata the one time. No one has ever believed me, but I ask you, in honor of our debt, to believe me now, my friend.

"I was no more than a boy, no older than my own lad is now, and it was a day much like this one. The fish were staying down, and I was hot and tired after a long day's effort for little reward. The lack of fish had forced me farther upstream than usual, and I was in waters previously unknown to me, in parts I had been warned from even approaching. But hungry bellies needed filling, and drove me even farther from home. So it was, as night fell, I found myself under the very same high tower we have so recently left behind.

"And here is where I need you to believe, my friend, for you have been in that same tower, and know the breadth and height of it. Believe me when I say that I saw Boitata, a snake bigger than any other snake in history, a snake that seemed to take forever to come up and out of the river, a snake that wound itself up and around the tower, in coils thicker than the thickest trees. She looked down at me, great golden eyes in the huge head that was at the highest point of that dark tower, even while her tail was still in the waters of the river."

*

And with that, Giraldo was indeed spent. He dropped back into the cot, his breathing hard and fast in little gasps. Banks would not have been greatly surprised to see steam coming out of the man's throat, such was the heat he generated. A great black vein pulsed in his neck, and the man's stared up at the canvas of the tent, once more unseeing.

For the first time in several minutes, Banks turned his attention away and back to the river. They were still traveling in the center, in the strongest part of the current, but it was getting close to dusk now, with dark shadows stretching across the surface from the trees on the left bank as the sun sank away to the west.

"Do you recognize anything, Wiggo?" he asked the private at the wheel. "Any clue how much longer until we reach the rig?"

To his surprise, it was Buller who answered.

"We're about 20 minutes away, I'd guess. There's a long sweeping turn ahead, then we'll be there."

Banks checked the sky and the position of the sun.

It was going to be touch and go whether they got back before it got full dark.

- 14 -

Banks took over the wheel for the last stretch, and Wiggins went to join Hynd and McCally for more coffee and a smoke. Buller sat in the belly of the boat under the canvas, keeping his thoughts to himself and staying silent. Giraldo's breathing got louder, seeming to take more effort, and the man's condition, while not appearing to be immediately fatal, wasn't getting any better either. The only thing that gave Banks hope was that the blackness in the veins in the guide's neck and chest did not seem to be spreading any faster.

He kept the power at full throttle, and concentrated on maintaining the boat's position in the center of the current as they negotiated the bend. There was enough light left as they turned the last curve to see the bulk of the dredger stretched out across the river ahead of them. The squad moved to prepare for docking without Banks having to prompt them, tidying away the stove, coffee, pot, and mugs and taking positions front and rear of the boat.

"Once we get to the dock, the sarge and Cally head inside and get kitted up first. Wiggo, you'll help me and get us tied up. When the other two get back, we'll get Giraldo here off and into a proper bed, I'll call for evac on the laptop link, and Cally can rustle up grub and a beer for us all while we wait. Everybody clear?"

There was no dissent, and they all moved quickly once Banks got the boat around the downstream side of the dredger and lined it up against the small dock.

"Buller, you wait here," he said as Hynd and McCally stepped out onto the docking area.

"Bugger that for a lark," Buller said. "This is my rig, and I'll do what I bloody well like."

Not for the first time, Banks considered tying the man up and gagging him for the duration, but Buller had already stepped up and out of the boat, and was hurrying along behind the other two men toward the living quarters.

*

Banks spent the next few minutes helping Wiggins get the boat tied up, then preparing Giraldo to move the sick man into the dredger's living quarters and a proper bed. Hynd and McCally were quick about getting kitted up and arrived back in their spare suits of camo gear and flak vests, rifles slung over their shoulders.

"All clear?" Banks asked.

"Just as we left it. But yon sneaky wee bugger we rescued is on the blower back home already, Cap," McCally said. "He's up to something."

"Aye? Well, so am I," Banks replied. "But first, let's get this man inside and into a real bed. It's the least we can do for him."

The four of them each took a corner of the cot and, carrying it like a stretcher, got the sick man out of the boat and across the dredger deck to the main living area. The guide moaned softly, but the black veins were like tree roots through his chest and neck, pulsing darkly among the sweat. Banks had rarely seen a man more ill yet still alive.

"Hang on there, man," he said as they gently laid Giraldo in a bed in what looked like it might be Buller's own room. "Help will be here before you know it."

He turned back to the squad.

"Sarge, Cally, make a quick sweep, just to make sure we're still on our lonesome here. Then get back and we'll get some grub and a beer inside us while I call for evac."

"Fine fucking plan, Cap," Wiggins replied with a smile.

*

It only took Banks a couple of minutes to get into his gear, but once dressed, and with a gun at his shoulder, he realized he was no longer an escapee fleeing a field of battle: he was a soldier again, just like that. The ritual of dressing and arming himself flicked a switch in his thinking and the events of the previous 24 hours were starting to take on a dreamlike quality, already fading from mind. He let them go—moving ahead was the priority now.

By the time he got back to the kitchen area, McCally was already working at the stove, and Hynd was in the fridge, getting out the beer.

"Nothing to report on the rig, Cap," Hynd said. "All clear."

He handed Banks a cold bottle of local lager that went down quick and smooth. Banks took a second, but only sipped at it; the temptation was to neck it as fast as the first, but he needed a clear head, for the next few minutes at least.

Buller was noticeable by his absence.

"Where's the wanker?" he asked and Hynd motioned through toward the office area.

"Through there on the laptop. Still talking to somebody back home. He's awfy excited about yon vein of gold we saw; I got that much before he shut the door on me."

"Aye, well, the money side of things is his problem, not ours. I'll be happy if we get him back to base without any of us strangling the bugger."

Long minutes passed. McCally produced a steaming pot of spicy fish and vegetable stew, they all had another beer while eating, Banks made a check on Giraldo, who was still alive, but barely, and Hynd and Wiggo left for another tour of the facility, all before Buller emerged from the office. He went straight to the fridge, got himself a beer, and had a wide grin on his face when he turned back to Banks.

"I left the connection open. Your boss wants a word with you."

Looking at the man's smug smile, Banks knew even before he left the scullery that he wasn't going to enjoy the next few minutes.

*

"But sir, I've got a dying man here," Banks said five minutes later. "We don't have the time, or the gear, to babysit a rich wanker who's looking to get richer. It's not worth the risk."

The video connection wasn't great, what with the colonel's face often wavering in and out of a badly pixilated screen, but his orders came through clear enough on the audio.

"The word's come down from on high, lad," his commanding officer said. "They've called in some favors and we've got a pair of tooled-up local Brazilian Air Force choppers coming in to your position. E.T.A. four hours. One will get your sick man off and away to hospital, the other is for you. You're to use it to do what Buller tells you. The job is to secure the gold seam you found for Queen and Country and rich bastards everywhere. So you'll make sure it's secured. You have your orders. I'll expect a report when the job's done. Is that clear?"

Banks had already tried explaining the situation, twice now, but the colonel wasn't showing any sign of wavering, and Banks knew better than to push too hard, for his superior's temper was legendary. But he had to make one last try.

"I've told you, it's risky. This is another weird one, Colonel," he said. "There's some big bloody snakes up on yon hill."

"And you've got big bloody guns, and more firepower coming. Do your damned job, Captain, or I'll find somebody who will."

*

Hynd took one look at Banks' face when he returned to the kitchen and, without speaking, handed him another beer and a cigarette. Banks finished both, pointedly ignoring Buller, before telling the squad of the orders he'd got from the colonel.

"And you told him about the weird shite?" Hynd asked.

"Aye. All of it. But the gold trumps all of that. Your man here talked to his daddy, his daddy talked to a politician, the politician poked the colonel, and now we get to do babysitting duties while a bunch of other fuckers get rich."

"Same as it ever was. This wanker's really got that kind of clout?" Wiggins said.

"This wanker really has," Buller replied, and smirked again. "So get used to it. You're working for me for the duration. You're all drinking my beer anyway; this only makes it official."

Wiggins spoke to Banks.

"Can I no' give him a wee slap, Cap? Enough to shut him up for a while?"

"You'd have to get in the queue for that one, Wiggo," Banks replied. "But orders is orders, so we're going up shit creek again, as soon as the choppers get here and we get Giraldo to a doctor."

Buller looked up and smirked again.

"Four hours? He's got half that, at the most."

"You'd better hope you're wrong," Banks replied. "Because if the man dies before the doctor gets here, I'll let Wiggo give you that slap."

Banks was pleased to see signs of doubt in Buller's eyes as he turned away.

*

What he really wanted was another beer, and another smoke. He was dismayed to notice that the old habit was back as if it had never been gone. He forced the craving down for now and instead sent McCally and Wiggins out on another tour of the dredger before going to the bedroom to check on Giraldo.

Much to his surprise, the man was awake. The guide smiled up thinly from a face that was otherwise a mask of pain.

"I thank you for the bed, my friend," he said. "It is easier on my old bones than the cot."

"Don't speak. There's a chopper on its way. Hold on."

The guide smiled again, a great sadness in his eyes.

"I always wished to ride in one of those. But I am afraid it might be the last journey I ever take, and I might be too dead to appreciate it."

He reached out and a sweat-laden, burning-hot hand gripped Banks at the left wrist.

"I can feel the snake, my friend. It slithers and creeps through me, looking for its way out of the dark. Promise me you will do the right thing, if it gets out? I have spent enough time on this river as a man; I do not wish to live in it as a snake."

"That's the venom talking," Banks said. "Fight it."

Giraldo coughed, thick black phlegm oozing at his lips.

"We both know better, my friend," he said. "I see it in your eyes, in your heart. Promise me. One last favor for a dying man. Actually, I ask for two. Find my boy. Tell him I died thinking of him."

Banks didn't bother with any platitudes. He knew a dying man when he saw one; he'd seen far too many not to know. Instead, he patted his rifle, then gripped the guide's hot hand in his own.

"You have my word, my friend, on both matters."

*

The squad spent the next hours on patrols sweeping the perimeter, keeping an eye on Giraldo, and smoking an endless succession of cigarettes over a similarly endless flow of coffee in the kitchen and mess area. Banks kept the squad off the beer. Buller, after taunting them with a cold one, went quiet when Wiggins pointed his weapon at the man's chest.

"Do that again, lad. Go on, I dare you. You might be rich, and about to get richer, but a bullet doesn't give a fuck about your money."

After that, the company man sat in silence, and after a time fell into a restless sleep upright in his chair, still cradling a beer in his arms. Banks started to hope that they would see out the time until the chopper's arrived in peace, but all such hope was dashed when Wiggins and McCally left to do a sweep. It was less than a minute later when he heard Wiggins shout out.

"Heads up, lads. We've got incoming."

- 15 -

Gunfire echoed around the facility seconds after the shout. Buller woke with a start, spilling beer down his front. He jerked as if hit as another volley of shots rang out.

"Lock yourself in your office," Banks said sharply. "And don't come out until I say it's safe."

The company man scuttled away. Banks and Hynd left him to it and headed out toward the source of the shots. Wiggins and McCally stood on the open decking that stretched toward where they had docked the boat. They fired into a slithering, squirming mass of giant snakes that teemed over the vessel, tearing it apart in splintering cracks and flying pieces of wood.

McCally and Wiggins' efforts didn't seem to be slowing the attack down although their shots raised wounds that gushed black and thick in the dark, and the air filled with the same acrid oil and vinegar oil that was all too recognizable.

By the time Banks and Hynd joined the other two men, there was little left of the boat but floating debris. The shooting had at least accomplished something. Two dead snakes floated away downstream with the wreckage. Banks and Hynd had enough time to push their earplugs in, in anticipation of the firefight to come. The remainder of the snakes came out of the water, a score or more of them, as one headed straight for the squad.

*

"Get those mother fucking snakes off my mother fucking deck!" Wiggins shouted.

They all fired at once, three quick rounds per man, picking out the closest of the attackers and pumping enough holes in it to slow it down. It opened a mouth that looked like a cave, two six-inch long fangs catching and reflecting the light from the living quarters at their back. Banks put two bullets down the thing's throat and it fell in a heap. It oozed more of the black viscous fluid, and the sour tang in the air got stronger. Two more of the creatures slid forward to take the dead one's place, each of them at least 15 feet long and like the ones Banks had seen at the pyramid, as thick as a man's thigh at the widest point.

"Head shots only, lads," Banks shouted. "Don't waste ammo."

The two approaching snakes went down quickly enough with clean shots, but the others behind weren't in the mood to come in singles or pairs, and surged forward, a dozen or more all coming on fast at once. Banks put three bullets down the yawning throat of another, then had to take a step back to avoid a searching, slithering purple tongue as one of the beasts reached almost to his feet.

"Back up, lads, double time," he shouted. "Back to the door. Let's get them in a funnel."

He held position as long as he could to let the others retreat, pumping three-shot bursts as fast as he dared, having to dance and jump to avoid striking heads and fangs. The noise almost deafened him, and the stench of acid and oil tickled at his throat, threatening to bring on a gag reflex.

He'd kept count well enough to know when his mag was about to run empty and, not waiting to see if the squad had made the doorway, emptied his weapon into the head of the nearest snake, and turned for the door.

The squad was, as he'd guessed, ready and waiting. They

covered his retreat, firing to either side of him and parting to let him through behind them to give him time to reload.

The four stood inside the doorway of the living quarters, allowing the snakes to come forward, then stepped back as a unit, four paces into the hallway, so that the snakes would have to bunch up tight to come toward them.

After that, it was little more than a shooting gallery.

There didn't seem to be enough intelligence in the creatures for them to form a coherent strategy. They kept coming on, even as the squad blew heads and tongues and fangs to globs of flesh and dripping goop. The stink was even stronger now, causing Banks' eyes to water and making his head swim as if he'd taken too much liquor. The enclosed space was concentrating the effect.

"Back up again, lads," he shouted. "To the kitchen doorway and cleaner air."

There were only four snakes left by the time they reached the doorway and they immediately felt the benefit of cleaner air. Two went down quickly, blasted to dripping gore. A third proved tougher to handle, and slid out a tongue that grabbed McCally by the leg and coiled tight like the grip of an octopus tentacle, trying to tug the man off his feet. Wiggins stepped to one side, put the barrel of his weapon against the thing's right eye, and fired three times. The snake went down, but McCally had to take some time to untangle himself from the still-coiled tongue around his calf. With two men momentarily out of the action, the last of the snakes, the biggest specimen they'd seen, made a lunge forward. It was so long that its tail was still outside the main door even as it came into the kitchen. Its head was almost as wide as the doorway itself, two red eyes fixed straight at Banks as it reared to strike.

The snake's mouth opened, and Banks tasted hot vinegar and oil again as he raised his weapon. At the same moment, Hynd stepped under the rearing head, put his rifle under its jaw, and fired. Banks put a shot into each eye for good measure but the thing was dead already as it fell to join the others in the carnage on the floor.

*

Banks' ears rang for long seconds after the firing, but he made out Wiggins' shout clear enough.

"Is that all of these buggers?"

"Go and check. Take Cally and have a keek out the main door," he shouted back. "Shout if there's any more of the fuckers. And don't do anything stupid."

"You know me, Cap,"

"Aye. That's the problem, Wiggo."

McCally and Wiggins left, stepping gingerly over the oozing bodies.

"Sarge, tell the wanker he can come out now. I'll go check on Giraldo."

Banks headed for the bedroom. As he reached the open door and stepped inside, he heard Wiggins shout from out in the corridor.

"Cap? You have to see this shite."

But Banks couldn't reply. His breath had caught in his throat at the sight of the thing on the bed where he'd left the guide.

It lay in a thick coil in the center on top of the sheets, a snake almost as big as the largest one they'd seen so far. A wide, flat head turned so that it looked straight at Banks.

It had Giraldo's eyes.

*

The head dipped and rose again, and a thick purple tongue slid wetly between the fangs that were starting to emerge from bloody gums. It made a rasping noise, deep in its throat, then repeated the sound, this time with its mouth open wider and the forked tongue moving rapidly. He realized it was trying to speak, and he finally recognized the single word being formed.

Promise.

He stepped forward, weapon raised.

"Aye, I did, man. I'm so sorry."

He put the weapon to the middle of the wide head, between the eyes. Giraldo, what little bit was left of him, looked up, and pressed his head tight against the barrel. Banks nodded, and fired twice.

He had already turned away as the coiled body slithered from the bed onto the floor and lay still.

- 16 -

He met Hynd and Buller standing in the kitchen doorway. They stood looking down at a body at their feet. When Banks had gone into the bedroom, there had been a huge dead snake there. Now there was a naked dead man, one with the back of his head blown out and blood, still wet, running red around the body.

"This is fucking weird, even for us, Cap," Hynd said.

"It's their leader," Buller added, and at first Banks didn't understand, until he bent and had a closer look at the dead man. There was no doubt about it. Despite the bullet wounds, Banks saw it was the tall one who'd led the occupants of the temple complex in their earlier capture.

"How did he get here?" Hynd said.

"I think they probably swam," Banks replied.

McCally spoke from out in the hallway.

"They're all like that, Sarge," he said. "All the fucking snakes are now dead people, men and women both. How the fuck does that work?"

"I'll be buggered if I know, lad, but I'd feel better if we got these bodies out of here." He turned to Buller. "Where do you keep the gasoline?"

*

Ten minutes later, they stood in the docking area watching the bodies burn. They'd dragged each one out individually, then piled them in a pyre on the deck by the waterside. Banks had them put Giraldo, now man again for the last time, on the top, then they doused the whole lot in gasoline and set it alight. They had to stand back as the pyre went up with a whoosh and surge that threatened to singe their eyebrows.

Nobody felt like speaking, and they all stood in silence. The burning went fast and furious, the bodies being rendered to ash and bone in a matter of minutes. When the flames finally started to die down, Wiggins stepped forward and kicked at the pile. It tumbled over into the river with a distinct hiss, and dispersed quickly, leaving only an oily scum on the surface to show for the lives of the dead. Even that was quickly dispersed, and soon the only sign they had ever been was a burned scar on the deck where the pyre had been.

Banks headed back inside, not for the beer, but for a drop of something harder. He fetched the bottle he'd seen earlier from the office, took it through to the mess area, and poured them all, even Buller, a finger of Scotch.

"To Giraldo, the poor auld bugger," he said, and knocked the whisky back in one. He took a pack of cigarettes from the table, lit a smoke, and stashed the rest of the packet and lighter in his pocket before turning to Buller.

"The choppers will be here inside the hour," he said. "We can all go home, right now, and be back in Scotland with a breakfast fry up and a pot of tea before you know it."

Buller finished his own drink before replying.

"We're not going back without the gold. Don't you see? It's even easier now. You've killed most of them. I never saw more than 20 at the temple, and you put that many down here tonight. The place will be empty. All we've got to do is waltz in, make sure everything's quiet, and sit on it. All that gold we saw is ours for the taking."

"If we get a vote, I'd rather have the fry up," Wiggins said.

Buller smiled again, that same eminently punchable smirk that Banks was coming to loathe.

"This isn't a fucking democracy," he said, addressing Banks. "You've got your orders. I'm in charge here."

"Look around you," Wiggins replied. "You couldn't manage a fuck in a brothel."

"That's enough, Wiggo," Banks said. "The man's right on one thing, we've got our orders. Go and be a soldier. You and Cally walk the perimeter and make sure there's no more buggering snakes about. The sarge and I will babysit the wanker for a bit."

Buller looked like he wanted to be offended, but wouldn't meet Bank's gaze and went to sit in his office without another word.

Hynd picked up the whisky bottle and waved it toward Banks with an eyebrow raised.

"No, put it away, Sarge," he replied. "Orders is orders. We've got to watch that bastard's back and get him back to yon temple. God help us."

"So what are we dealing with? Fucking shapeshifters?"

"I told you what I saw at the pyramid. You saw it for yourself just now, Sarge. And you saw what a bite did for Giraldo. So rule one: Don't get fucking bitten. We're going to get Buller to his temple, get it secured, then fuck off and leave him and his rich pals to it."

Hynd smiled thinly.

"As Wiggo would say, that sounds like a fucking plan to me."

*

The whop of approaching choppers sounded in the night air and the squad, with Buller at their back, were all outside waiting as the two craft approached and landed on the wide deck at the docking area. Banks saw that they were Russian-built, Mil Mi-24s, with Brazilian Air Force Insignia.

They waited for the rotors to stop, then greeted the crew as they disembarked. As Banks had guessed, the four pilots were all Brazilian, but their English was as good as Giraldo's had been, and he had no trouble briefing them in the kitchen. If they noticed the blood smears that the squad hadn't quite managed to clean up, they were too professional to make note of it.

"We were told there was a sick man to transport," their senior officer, a captain by his insignia, said. "We should send him back straight away before we talk anymore."

"He didn't make it," Banks said bluntly, and again the pilots were too professional to make anything of it. He explained the plan of action, and gave them a rundown of what would be waiting for them in the highlands at their destination. One of them made the sign of the cross and muttered a prayer under his breath at the mention of the temple in the highlands upriver.

"We'll go at first light," he said when he was done.

"Bugger that. We go now," Buller replied.

"No, we don't," Banks said. "You might be in charge, but that doesn't mean I'm going to allow you to get away with fucking stupidity. We are not going into a blind situation in the dark. I won't put my men at risk that way, orders or no orders."

"Then I'll see you busted back to private on our return, and I'll just take these local chaps. We'll go without you," Buller said, and looked to the Brazilian crew. Banks was pleased to see they were as professional as he'd expected.

"I'm afraid I must agree with Captain Banks," the chief officer said. "Going blind into the dark is something only an idiot would contemplate, especially on this river. We go in the morning."

Buller blustered and complained. He made threats. Then he tried offering bribes. All that got him was contempt, and once again, he left to sulk in his office.

"I do not think I like him very much," the Brazilian captain said.

"Then you and I should get along just fine," Banks replied, and got a grin in return.

Banks set up a watch schedule for what little was left of the night, and told the squad to get any rest they could manage.

"We've got a big day ahead of us, and I need us all sharp."

Dawn was approaching all too quickly.

- 17 -

Banks and Hynd took the last watch two hours before dawn. The sergeant went straight to the choppers for a closer look at them.

"They're old, but the Ruskies built these things to last. They'll get a job done," he said, looking at the mounted ordnance. "Half-inch Yak-B Gatling guns, carrying maybe 1500 rounds of ammo per gun. These rockets under the wings are 9K114 Shturm mounts, two-pound warheads, six missiles in each wing."

"Enough for a big bang then?" Banks said.

"Aye. We've enough between these two beasts for a lot of big bangs. These are normally anti-tank missiles. We've got enough to blow the top off yon temple and level the causeway back to base rock."

"I don't think that's what the colonel had in mind when he told us to secure the site," Banks replied with a grin. "But it'll be nice to have the option available if we need it."

They made a tour of the perimeter of the facility while smoking another cigarette each. The banks of the river on either side were dark lines of deeper shadow, and the river itself shone and shimmered under the blanket of stars with only wispy clouds passing quickly over to obscure the view.

"Do you think the wanker was right, Cap?" Hynd asked as they approached the docking deck on their return. "About us having got most of them already?"

Banks shrugged.

"Who knows?" he said. "I only saw about 20 or so myself, like he says. But that doesn't mean there's not more of the fuckers. And we know fuck all about these things. We don't know where they come from, whether they breed or not, or how big they get. Let's not have any assumptions in mind going in."

"Maybe they were all like Giraldo? Maybe you only get it by getting bit?"

"Maybe aye, maybe naw," Banks replied. "All we know is that they can be put down fast with a bullet or two. So as long as we're tooled up, and don't lose our rifles again, we can get the job done. Don't over think it, Sarge. I have a cunning plan. We get in, secure the site, and don't get dead."

*

Dawn came between the acts of them lighting another cigarette each and finishing it, a soft orange glow in the eastern sky that ate the night in a matter of minutes. On cue, biting insects started to swarm across the rippling surface of the river, and the day immediately warmed, a hot kiss full of promises of later fire.

Banks flicked his butt away and watched until the current took it away out of sight downstream.

"Time to go to work. Fetch the others, Sarge. Let's get this day started."

Within a few minutes, the squad were all out on the deck and ready to load the choppers with what little gear they had left.

"Who is traveling with who?" the Brazilian captain asked.

"Buller, you're in the second chopper," Banks said. "You'll hold off with them away from the main site until we get it secured. The rest of us will load up with the captain here and go in first."

"Nope, no way," Buller said. "This is my find. I'll be with you when you secure it. Remember, I'm in charge of this operation."

"We've had this discussion already," Banks said.

"And I gave in then. But not this time. There's no danger, I'm telling you. They're all fucking dead already."

"I'm all out of fucks to give for what you think," Banks replied. "So come with us, if that's what you want. But I'm not responsible if you screw up, agreed?"

He saw doubt in the other man's eyes, but the greed overrode it.

"Agreed," Buller said.

Banks played his high card.

"Okay then. Wiggo, you're on babysitting duty for the duration. Shoot him if he does anything that might jeopardize the rest of us. That's an order."

Wiggins' wide grin more than made up for Buller's surly demeanor as they loaded up into the first of the choppers.

*

After lift-off, the noise from the rotors precluded any conversation in the cabin. Wiggins sat opposite Buller, saying nothing, but grinning while staring straight at the man, which only made Buller squirm all the more.

"Suit up, lads," Banks shouted, and opened the kit bags.

Each man wore a light camouflage suit, to which they each added a helmet with an attached pair of night vision goggles. They all wore thin but sturdy waterproof boots and a lightweight flak jacket with pouches filled with spare magazines for their weapons.

And this time we won't be giving them away. No matter what comes at us.

Buller was the odd man out, wearing a thin shirt, canvas trousers, and sneakers on his feet. Banks found a flak jacket stowed under a seat and had Buller put it on. He still wished he could leave the man behind; having a civilian along complicated matters.

But I got an order. I'll follow it. I'm a soldier—it's what I do.

He went up front and motioned that he wanted to talk. The captain passed him a headset so they could communicate privately. He had to take off his own helmet to wear it, but after a test could hear the captain clearly.

"If you have to hover, how long can you stay?" he asked.

"An hour, Captain, no more than that. But you said the area has an open roadway of paved stone? Landing should not be a problem."

"It's the taking off again that has me worried," Banks replied, but didn't elaborate. His attention was drawn to the view out of the main window to the front of the pilots. The jungle, a carpet of infinite shades and hues of green, lay across from horizon to horizon with the river winding through it, a great shining snake leisurely going about its business with no concern for the world of men. The only thing breaking above the flat expanse of greenery was a series of rocky outcrops on the far horizon, getting closer so fast that Banks could already make out the pyramid that market the highest point.

"Five minutes," the Brazilian captain said.

*

The two choppers circled the temple complex 100 feet above the top of the pyramid. There was no sign any life, no sign of any movement at all. They did two passes to be sure, then the chopper captain had his second craft move to an outcrop a mile away to the north that was big enough for a landing. He turned to Banks and pointed to the widest part of the causeway that ran along the ridge of the hill.

"I will set down there," he said. "And I will only take off if we come under sustained attack. We will wait for your return there. We have got your back, Captain."

Banks gave him a thumbs-up, handed back the headset, and went back to his seat for the landing.

It went smoothly and without a hitch. A minute later, the chopper was on the ground, and the squad was getting out of the vessel. The captain passed Banks the same headset they'd used earlier. After a few seconds, he figured out how he could clip the piece to his ear so that he could wear both headset and helmet. Once he was happy that any sudden movement wouldn't lead to the loss of either, the pilot spoke at his ear.

"This is good for 100 meters line of sight," he said. "It will not work well in a building or through rock, but we will be here and ready to come to your aid if you call for it."

Banks gave him another thumbs up, and jumped to the ground, running out from under the rotors to join the squad on the causeway.

*

The whump of the rotors slowed and ceased when the captain switched off, and Banks was able to speak normally, keeping his voice low as he directed the squad.

"I want a sweep of everything above ground here first," he said. "Wiggo and Buller with me on the left, Sarge and Cally on the right, and join up at the foot of yon pyramid. Shoot first, question later, and shout if you find anything hinky."

Buller spoke up, almost shouting.

"We need to get down to the cave with the gold, right now."

"No," Wiggo replied, barely above a whisper, but leaning in close to Buller's face so that his meaning could not be any clearer. "What we need is for you to be a good wanker, shut the fuck up, keep quiet, and not get us killed. Or do you want a skelp?"

Buller wisely went quiet, and followed, sandwiched between Banks and Wiggins, as they headed left toward the first of the tumbled ruins that lined the causeway.

- 18 -

Banks moved slowly toward the nearest doorway opening. The sun was already climbing high, throwing the inside of the building into shadows that were almost black. He switched on the light on his rifle and stepped cautiously forward.

He'd expected crude living quarters, or possibly a storage area for food, so what he found inside surprised him.

The first hint was when his gun's light reflected back, yellow and gold, from the wall directly ahead. He moved the light around. He had walked into a room some 12 feet square and eight feet high, and every inch of wall and roof was covered in tiles, squares of eight inches each, and all, by the look of it, carved in thick, solid slabs of gold.

Wiggins whistled as he followed Banks and Buller inside.

"What the fuck is this now, Cap? Fucking Eldorado?"

"Maybe it is at that," Buller said, and Banks turned to see if the man was joking, but he looked deadly serious.

"Legends usually start somewhere in fact," Buller added.

"Tell me about it," Banks replied. He shone his rifle barrel's light around, but there was nothing in the room apart from the carvings on the wall.

"Wait," Buller said. "Hold the light steady and let me have a closer look."

There was little sign of the smugness he'd shown earlier; there was now only a wide-eyed face of childlike wonder. For once,

Banks could completely understand what the other man was feeling. He did as requested and held the light steady over a patch of the wall. Buller studied it closely.

"I'm no expert," the man said after a few minutes. "But this looks like some kind of story, maybe a history."

"If so, it's one that'll have to wait until we're secure," Banks replied. "Wiggo, next building. Let's make this a quick sweep. I don't want us to be still fucking about here when it gets dark again."

*

The next building was tumbled in ruin, the roof long gone and only fragments of the walls left standing but they were amazed to see more of the gold tiles, lying, discarded in piles on the ground, with vines and roots growing through them.

"They've got so much of it. It has no value to them," Buller said in a hushed voice, as if the very idea of it appalled him.

"Well it's no' as if they're going to be down the club on a Saturday night blowing the lot on booze, blow, strippers and fags, is it?" Wiggins replied. "Although maybe we should get the kit bags from the chopper and fill them up with some of these wee shiny tiles, Cap? Might help with our pensions?"

Banks laughed.

"Sounds like a fucking plan to me, Wiggo. Maybe on the way back," he said. "But first let's make sure this place is as dead as it feels."

'Dead' was exactly how it felt. If Banks hadn't known better, he'd have said that no one had been here except themselves for many years. It had that same sense of empty loss that he often got from visiting remote and abandoned homesteads back in the Highlands of home. The weather was better here, and they didn't have mounds of gold tiles just lying around unclaimed in the

Scottish hills, more's the pity, but he felt the same sense of sadness and longing for a past long gone in this place that he did across the sea.

That feeling was exacerbated the farther along the causeway they traveled. There was more gold, more tumbled ruin, and still no sign that any of the buildings had ever actually been lived in. He remembered the tighter-packed buildings they'd passed on the track along the far side of the hill on that first night, and wondered if they'd need to sweep that area too, or whether that would be just as empty and dead as this.

He looked across to the other side of the pathway and saw that Hynd and McCally had advanced almost up to the steps of the pyramid, 20 yards or so ahead of Bank's threesome.

"Wiggo," he said. "Get a shift on. Time's a wasting here."

They hurried past the last tumbled building, pausing only long enough to make sure it was more of the same mixture of aged ruin and scattered gold, and met Hynd and McCally at the foot of the pyramid steps.

"All clear on your side, Sarge?" he asked.

"Aye," Hynd replied. "But there's enough gold to buy Aberdeen twice and still have change."

"Same over here," Banks replied. He tapped at his ear and spoke to the chopper captain. "All clear so far. We're heading inside the pyramid to check that out so we might go dark. Watch our backs."

"We're right here and not going anywhere until you get back, Captain," came the reply, then Banks led the squad, with Buller in the middle, up the steep stairs of the pyramid.

*

Like their first ascent, it proved to be hard going. Buller, not having the benefit of their military-grade fitness, struggled after the first few steps, and they were forced to keep a snail's pace to cater for him.

"We shouldn't even be going this way," the businessman complained at the approximate halfway point of the climb, where he had to stop for a rest. "The gold seam's down in the cave far below."

"Securing the site means securing the whole site," Banks replied. "Not only the shiny, expensive bits."

"There's naebody here. An idiot could see that."

Wiggins stepped up close to the man.

"Are you calling the captain here an idiot?"

"That's not what I meant..." Buller blustered. "I'm just saying..."

"And I'm just telling you. Last time. Shut the fuck up or you'll get a skelp."

Buller looked from Wiggins to Banks, and back to Wiggins. The private winked at him, and smiled.

"What's it to be?"

Buller went back to climbing.

*

Banks waited on the top step for Buller to catch up. He tapped at his ear and spoke, looking down the length of the causeway to where the chopper sat quiet at the far end.

"Everything still okay down there?" he asked.

"All quiet, Captain. I think we're the only ones here."

"Let's hope so," he said. "Checking out now. Will check back in when I can."

Buller heaved himself up the last step, stopped, and looked around.

"Well, you got us up here. Now what?"

"Now we go down through the dungeon we were held in

before," Banks said. "I need to make sure it's empty. And it'll get us to your cave soon enough. What has me worried is that those people, when they weren't being bloody big snakes, must have lived somewhere, eaten somewhere, and we haven't found that yet. I won't be happy until then. So into the pyramid we go, to see what's what.

"But first, I need to warn you. If nobody's been here since the night before last, then your man Wilkes will be inside here. And it's not pretty."

Buller waved a hand as if pushing the words away.

"It won't be anything I haven't already seen. I told you before, they made me watch."

"It's your funeral," Banks said.

"No. It's Wilkes'. But he got paid well enough, so fuck him."

"Nobody gets paid well enough for this," Banks said, and led them into the altar room at the top of the pyramid.

*

Wilkes' body was still splayed out on the altar. A swarm of bloated black flies crawled over it feasting in so thick a carpet that the body appeared to squirm in the throes of a fit.

"Well, that's fucking disgusting," Wiggins said.

Before Banks could counsel caution, the private stepped forward, and rolled the body off the altar. The swarm of flies rose lazily in the air and started to dissipate almost immediately. Wiggins went over to the wall and Banks saw that the cauldron of oil still sat there in the corner. Wiggins bent toward it, obviously intent on using the contents to burn the body. He didn't get as far as lifting it, for the room echoed with the sound of rock grinding on rock. They had to step back as the altar stone slid across the floor, slowly with loud grinding and the crash and clatter of wood on wood somewhere under their feet.

Seconds later, they stood looking down into a dark hole below them. A run of stone steps led away, down into the darkness.

- 19 -

"I guess we're back to the Indiana Jones shite then?" Wiggins said.

Banks leaned forward, switched on his gun light and waved the beam down the newly exposed steps. At the same time, he smelled something all too familiar. It wasn't strong, but it was distinctive, the odor of vinegar and burnt oil.

"We don't have time for stumbling around in the dark. We need to get to the fucking gold," Buller protested again when Banks stepped down onto the first of the stairs, but the man went quiet when Wiggins prodded him in the back with his gun barrel. All five of them descended in step into the darkness below.

Banks took point, keeping his light steady ahead so that he could always see where he was putting his feet. It was even warmer here than it had been out in the heat of the day. It wasn't humid, rather being a stifling dry heat that felt like he was breathing fire. The tang of oil and vinegar got stronger as they descended. After a few feet, they passed the mechanism that worked the pivot for moving the altar, a complex set of wooden gears, ropes, and pulleys that looked almost too rotten to be functional. Banks studied it only long enough to ensure there wouldn't be a trap sprung at their back then continued the descent.

Even Buller knew well enough to keep quiet, and they went down in silence, into what was quickly becoming an oppressive heat and stench. Banks was considering retracing their steps in search of better air when he felt a breath of breeze in his face, and a cooler one at that. The sound of his footfalls, which had been dull slaps, now took on an echoing, wider quality, and as he suspected, they arrived at the bottom of the stairwell soon afterward, to be faced with a dark, open area ahead that his rifle light wasn't quite powerful enough to penetrate.

There was another smell here too, even above the tang of vinegar and oil. It took Banks a few seconds to recognize it, as he hadn't been expecting it here in the dark, but it too was unmistakable once identified. It was an almost meaty taste of human body sweat.

He pulled down the night vision goggles and switched them on.

He immediately wished he hadn't.

*

They stood in the doorway of another square chamber, this one being the biggest so far. Like the others, this one was covered wall and ceiling with more of the carvings, the same size as the tiling they'd seen outside, although here they were done, not in gold, but in stone as ancient as that which made up the pyramid steps outside. And also unlike the buildings outside, this place was most definitely occupied.

The room was some 30 feet square. Bodies sat, backs straight, legs outstretched, all seated close to each other around all of the walls. There was a thin, whistling noise and Banks realized it was breathing, all of them, some 50 individuals at his best count, breathing in and out in unison.

They appeared to be a mixed population, old and young, man and woman, but all of them stark naked sitting there in the dark, breathing together and staring, wide-eyed into emptiness.

"What is it?" Buller whispered from behind him. "What can

you see?"

Banks realized the man was the only one of them without the benefit of the night goggles. He stepped closer to the nearest wall and shone his light in the face of the nearest sitting figure. The woman, middle-aged and as pale as alabaster, didn't so much as blink. Buller yelped in fear, the first sign of any emotion he'd shown, but Banks couldn't really blame him for it.

"Bloody hell, Cap," Wiggins whispered in the dark. "What kind of shite have you led us into this time?"

Buller answered.

"We need to kill them," he said. "We need to kill them all, right now."

"Bugger that for a lark," Wiggins said. Banks hushed him to quiet and pulled Buller back into the doorway, getting up close and keeping his voice soft and low.

"I'm not here to murder civilians for you," he said.

"Civilians? Who said anything about fucking civilians? These aren't people, you idiot. Don't you see? They're fucking snakes, and they're hiding from the sun in here waiting for night."

As soon as Buller mentioned it, Banks knew the man had to be right. He left the doorway and went back over toward the woman, getting as close to her as he had to Buller seconds before. Up close it was obvious, especially when he lifted the goggles and studied her under the light from his rifle.

Her pupils had a slit running down the iris, yellow and golden, and the veins at her neck pulsed as blackly as the ones he'd seen on Giraldo before the change came over him. She didn't blink, even when he shone the light directly in her eyes, although a thin, forked tongue slid from between her lips and she hissed as she breathed.

Banks moved to the man beside her; he had exactly the same symptoms, down to the slithering tongue when light was shone in his eyes. Banks backed away to the squad in the doorway.

"For once, it seems that this wanker's right," he said. "They're all infected."

"It's not an infection," Buller said. "It's some kind of magic."

"Fucking snake magic bullshit," Wiggins said. "Aye, that'll be right."

Once again, Banks hushed them into quiet.

"Whatever it is, we're getting out of here. About turn."

Buller almost shouted.

"We can't leave yet. We need to kill them."

"Not going to happen," Banks said softly. "This is a job for doctors, not soldiers."

"I demand you kill these fuckers," Buller said, and this time he shouted. It rang and echoed in the chamber. The cadence of the heavy breathing around them got faster, and in one of the corners, something heavy moved.

"If you don't shut the fuck up, right now, I'll shoot you in the knee and leave you down here with them," Wiggins whispered, and even through the night goggles, Banks saw the blood leave Buller's face and the fear grow in his eyes.

"You wouldn't dare," he whispered back.

"Just fucking try me," Wiggins replied.

When Hynd and McCally led them back upstairs, Buller hurried behind them, as if keen to put plenty of space between himself and Wiggins.

*

Banks had them stop only as they approached the exit hole back up to the altar room.

"Cally, you're up," he said, pointing to the rotting timbers of the gear mechanism. "Can you rig this somehow so that it will close at our backs, and stay closed unless we fuck about with it from above?"

McCally cast an eye over the mechanism.

"Give me the sarge and five minutes and we'll see what we can do?"

"Get to it then," Banks said. "But keep your eye on the stairwell. Once these fuckers start to move, they move fast."

He led Buller and Wiggins up into the altar room, then out onto the top of the pyramid where they sucked in some welcome fresher air.

"You're making a big mistake," Buller said as Banks handed Wiggins a cigarette and they both lit up.

"Maybe," Banks said. "But I'm a soldier, not a murderer, and I'm not about to start now, snakes or no snakes. Not when I can trap them down there, and do this."

He tapped at his ear and called up the chopper pilot.

"Still here," he said.

"I am pleased to hear it, Captain," the reply came. "Site secured?"

"We've still got more of a sweep to do," he replied. "But I need a favor. I need you to get a medical team on standby to come in as soon as we give the all clear. We've got some kind of contagion among the locals here that's going to need a lot of help."

The pilot didn't ask any questions, accepting Banks' word.

"I will make the call as soon as you check off, Captain."

"Thank you," Banks replied. "I'll check back in within the hour. Hopefully, it's all plain sailing from here on in."

*

"I still think this is a mistake," Buller said as they went back into the altar room.

"Aye, we heard you already," Wiggins replied. "My offer still stands if you want a bullet in the knee or a skelp."

Buller didn't get time to reply as McCally and Hynd came up

the steps into the room. McCally held a thick, frayed rope that stretched back down the hole.

"Give this a hard tug, then let go," he said, handing it to Banks. "Then cross your fingers. That shit down there's as rotted as my old grannie's front teeth. I cannae guarantee it's going to take the weight."

"Stand back then," Banks said, and pulled hard on the rope. He heard a loud clunk below them, wood against wood, and let go of the rope at the same time as it was pulled hard from his hand. The sound of rock grinding on rock echoed around them, and the altar stone slid slowly back into place. As if from a distance, they heard crunching and splintering as wood split and something below tumbled away down the stairwell.

"The proverbial spanner in the works," McCally said with a smile. "Nobody's coming back up unless we shove this block of stone out the way from up here."

"Good job, Cally," Banks said. "Take five and have a fag. Then we'll head down below, and get this wanker his cave of gold."

- 20 -

The top run of steps down the passage at the rear of the altar room were still slippery with oil, but the rest of the descent went without a hitch. They wound their way down, firstly to the cells where they'd been held earlier, then descended in the dim winding stairwell. Now that it was daylight outside, they had enough light coming in the slits of the windows to show them the steps ahead. They didn't meet any resistance all the way to the foot of the stairs and arrived in the cavern minutes later.

The first thing that Banks noticed was that there was no body on the floor in the doorway. The dead man was gone.

"I ken he didn't get up and walk," Wiggins said. "You cut his chest and belly to ribbons then burned his insides out. So where did the buggering thing go?"

"Eaten, is my guess," Buller said. "Eaten by his pals. They're fucking big snakes. It's what fucking big snakes do."

It wasn't the floor where Buller had his attention focused, but on the ceiling and walls of the cavern. Now, with more light available and daylight streaming in the doorway, the extent of the seam was even more impressive. The wide band ran, six feet thick in places, fully across the whole extent of the chamber.

"I'm going to be as rich as fucking Croesus. This could go all the way up through the hill," Buller said in whispered awe. "It's probably why they built the temple here in the first place."

"I doubt that," Banks said in reply. "You saw the rooms up on the causeway. They didn't worship the gold; they treated it as something to use in building work, a canvas for their stories."

"It must be the gold. Why else would they put such a bloody huge temple in the middle of the Amazonian jungle?"

"You said it yourself," Banks said. "Some kind of snake worship. Magic, I believe was the word you used? There's something else here we haven't got to the bottom of yet."

Buller wasn't paying attention. He was already walking away across the cavern, charting the course of the gold seam with a raised hand. Banks left him to it and went to the doorway before tapping at his ear again.

"Banks checking in," he said. The Brazilian captain came back loud and clear in his ear.

"Glad to hear you safe and sound," the pilot said. "Nothing to report up here; all quiet on the causeway."

"Let's hope it stays that way. We'll be with you in 10 minutes. I want to check this outer track here. If we make it back okay, then you can go ahead and call in that medical team. Looks like the site is secure."

"What about the fucking huge snakes, Cap?" Wiggins said when Banks stepped back into the cavern.

"If the theory is right, and they're all infected people, then we've got them trapped down there in the dark under the pyramid. If any others turn up, you have my permission to shoot the fuck out of them. I've had about enough sneaking about in this place to do me for a while. Let's do a reccy up the hill, then we can leave this wanker with his gold and get the fuck off this hill. Whatever happens next is his problem, not ours."

"We need to get more people out here," Buller said. "Geologists, engineers…"

"Doctors first, for those poor bastards we left down in the dark," Hynd said.

"I told you, they can't be helped."

Wiggins stood up close to Buller again.

"And I told you to shut the fuck up. They'll be helped. You might be a murdering fuckwit, but that's not how we do things in this squad."

Buller's mouth looked like it wanted to work, but Wiggins shook a finger in the man's face.

"Nope. Just nope. Keep it zipped. One more word out of you and I really will put a bullet in you. That's a promise, from one Scots bastard to another."

*

The squad, with a silent Buller in the middle, moved out a minute later onto the track that wound around the hill. They'd headed down to the river the last time but now Banks led them upward, toward the ridge they could see up a steep slope ahead of them.

The track was so narrow they had to climb single file, and it was precipitous in the extreme in places, with a sheer drop to their right, 100 feet and more to the canopy of the rainforest below. Banks led, searching the ground ahead for tracks or any sign that someone might have recently passed this way. He was so intent that he almost didn't notice when a sprinkle of dry earth fell on him from higher up. He reacted immediately, instinct kicking in, and looked up, his weapon already aimed along his line of sight. There was no target, only more dirt, now accompanied by pebbles and increasingly larger stones. The track underfoot trembled and bucked, threatening to throw them all down the cliff face.

"Earthquake!" he shouted, then had no time for words as the path lifted several inches and then fell back, leaving a sick emptiness in Banks' stomach and a split second sensation of falling, then relief when his feet planted on solid—or nearly so—

ground. He turned his head, and saw the squad hugging the rock face. Buller had almost taken the tumble off the edge, and Wiggins had him by an arm, pulling him back up onto the track to where he could at least get onto his hands and knees.

The tremor stopped as quickly as it started. Some more fine dirt fell in their hair, then everything went silent save for some surprised parakeets that circled overhead, squawked loudly for a few seconds then dropped to settle in their roosts, hidden in the canopy. Buller looked white-faced and wide-eyed, and trembled so badly he might have been in the throes of a fit.

"If you're going to spew, don't do it on my boots," Wiggins said.

Buller got carefully to his feet.

"Thanks," he said, but didn't look Wiggins in the eye.

"Don't mention it. Really, don't mention it."

Banks' headset crackled and the pilot's voice came over the com.

"Still there, Captain?"

"Aye, just about," Banks replied. "All okay up there?"

"We were in a clear enough spot to be away from any trouble," he replied. "Just as well you got out of the pyramid though. It looks like it has caved in at the top level."

Banks had the sinking feeling in his gut again, but it wasn't the earthquake that did it this time.

"Take off," he said. "No questions, get in the air right now. And keep an eye on the pyramid. You might have an attack incoming."

-21-

Banks set off up the path at a flat run, knowing that the squad would follow his lead. The track was rough and got steeper the closer he got to the top, so much so that he was breathing heavily and over-heating as he crested the ridge. He looked down the causeway, saw, and heard, the rotors of the chopper start up, then turned to face the pyramid.

The cube-shaped altar room that had sat on top of the structure had fallen inward on itself, the roof lying in two pieces on the steps some 10 feet below, and there was no sign of the altar itself. Banks' heart fell again when he saw a large stone seeming to move of its own volition, and wasn't surprised to see the head of one of the big snakes come up out of the rubble and taste the air. It fixed its gaze on the chopper, attracted either by the movement or the sound of the rotors. It pulled the whole length of its body up and out of the hole at the top of the pyramid and slithered down the steps.

A second snake followed it immediately afterward, and a third. The chopper still wasn't up to full power and Banks saw that the snakes would be on it before it was ready to take off.

He ran down a slight incline and put himself between the first snake and the aircraft, already raising his weapon as he came to a stop. The snake wasn't moving as fast as the ones they had faced on the dredger the night before. He had time to wonder whether the relative sluggishness might be due to it being daylight, then had to pay full attention as the creature was almost upon him, with two more right behind it, and at least six coming down the pyramid steps behind those.

The snake lunged, mouth opening and fangs dripping. Banks took two steps back, aimed and fired in one swift movement, three rounds down its gullet that dropped it like a stone. The other two came forward fast, but by that time McCally was at his side and between them they put the snakes down quickly and efficiently. Banks paused long enough to force his earplugs into place; the sound of gunfire and the rise of the rotor noise were already proving to be deafening.

Then it was all shooting and defending as a swarm of the snakes slithered down from the pyramid, seething and roiling in a mass that made it hard to distinguish one from another. Hynd and Wiggins joined in and the four men of the squad pumped bullets into the wriggling flesh. From the corner of his eye Banks saw the chopper lift up and away.

He motioned for the squad to start backing up.

"Let's see if we can funnel these bastards the same way we did at the dredger," he shouted and stepped backward toward the doorway of the nearest intact building. Buller was also already on the move to the same spot, backing off fast.

The rolling mass of snakes kept pace with them, leaving a trail of discarded skin, torn flesh, and gore in a slimy trail behind it. The air smelled of gunshot, warm vinegar, and oil. The squad kept firing and kept backing off toward the doorway.

The snakes kept coming.

*

Banks reached the door first and pushed Buller deeper into the gold-lined room. Banks' plan was again the simplest one; funnel the snakes so that they could only attack one at a time, and pick them off. So far, the beasts, despite their obviously human origins, showed no signs of being intelligent enough to see the senselessness of their attack. Banks was also aware of the irony of the situation. These were the same things, albeit transformed, that he had refused to kill in the chamber under the pyramid. Now he was only too happy to see them put down to a violent death. He knew, from bitter experience, that the scene would be relived in the depths of night in the months, even years, to come. But for now, there was only the adrenaline rush, the shooting, and the death as snakes filled the doorway with the bullet-ridden bodies of their dead.

"I'm running low," McCally shouted. "Stepping out."

Banks was close to having the same issue himself. And the snakes kept coming, now having to push their way through and over the dead piling in the doorway. The noise in the enclosed space pounded and rang, vibrating through every bone in his body, the earplugs doing little to lessen the impact. His headphone buzzed, and the chopper pilot shouted. It was only one phrase, but it was enough to get Banks smiling.

"Fire in the hole."

*

"Everybody down," Banks shouted. He threw himself to the floor and was pleased to see that Buller at least had enough good sense to join them. At almost the same moment, the snakes piled beyond the doorway were blown to chunks of flesh, bone, and gore as the twin Gatling guns of the chopper made a strafing run along the causeway outside.

"Stay down. Coming back 'round," the pilot said at Banks' ear. The floor shook, not earthquake this time but four explosions, almost simultaneous, and the doorway lit up in a brilliant flare of white, then yellow then red.

The sound echoed and rang for seconds afterward, then everything fell quiet save for the slightly distant sound of the chopper rotors. Banks' headset buzzed again.

"All clear, Captain," the pilot said. "For now, at least."

Banks stood, somewhat groggy from the assault of sound and vibration. He put two bullets in the head of a snake on the doorway that was still squirming, trying to get at him, then stepped over it, and out into a scene of carnage.

*

Dead snakes, or at least the few remaining pieces of them, lay strewn and scattered the length of the causeway. The main concentration of blasted flesh was around the doorway he'd left, but oozing, stinking, remains stretched from where Banks stood all the way to the steps of the pyramid. The stench was worse than anything he'd ever experienced, the tang of hot vinegar and oil setting his guts rolling and tumbling. When Hynd offered him a cigarette, he accepted it gratefully and let the smoke mask the worst of it.

"I don't think any of these buggers will be changing back again," Hynd said laconically.

"They're going to be in a hell of a mess if they do," Banks agreed.

The chopper made a pass overhead and Banks gave the pilot a wave of thanks.

"No problem, Captain," the pilot said at his ear. "We are glad to be of help. Shall we come and get you?"

"Give me two minutes to check all's clear," Banks replied.

Banks had the squad make a tour of the causeway, checking that all of the snakes were indeed destroyed, although, given the carnage, it was obvious that the job had already been done.

"So, is the site secure enough for you yet?" Buller said, his sarcasm all too clear.

"Aye, it is," Banks said. "We'll be fucking off now. It's all yours. We'll take the lead chopper, and you can wait with the backup for your team to get here."

"Wait. We didn't bring any provisions. What will I eat?"

"Snake?" Banks said, and turned away before the temptation to punch the man really did get too much to bear.

*

He was about to call down the chopper to evacuate the squad when McCally called from the doorway where the dead snakes were already starting to rot down under the full heat of the day. The flesh bubbled and seethed, a disgusting hybrid mixture of snakeskin and human tissue, gray and red and black and oozing. Banks was glad he still had the cigarette at hand as he walked over.

"There's something happening inside, Cap. You need to see this. It's really fucking weird."

"Weirder than fucking giant snake people who live in a pyramid?"

"You tell me, boss."

Banks followed the corporal back into the cubical room. The walls appeared to be melting, the carvings losing their definition, turning smooth as the gold slid, like an over-application of fresh paint, down the walls in drips that became runnels that became rivulets. The two of them had to stand back as it started to drip from the ceiling. He hadn't taken note of it before, but the floor was slightly concave, running to a small, almost unnoticeable hole in the center. The melted gold found its way down toward it, and a glowing river ran away to somewhere underground.

And the process was definitely accelerating.

- 22 -

"Out here, Cap," Wiggins shouted. "What the fuck is this shite now?"

Out to one side of the building, the private had picked up one of the fallen gold tiles. What was left of it now ran through his fingers, dripping toward the ground.

"I only wanted a wee souvenir," Wiggins said, as the last of the gold dripped and ran off his little finger. He showed Banks his hands. They were completely clean.

"It's the same over here, Cap," Hynd called out from the other side of the causeway. "It's all running away, heading off somewhere under us."

"It's some fucking weird chemical reaction to those bloody bombs you dropped. It must be. If we lose this find, it's your fucking fault. The seam. We need to check the seam," Buller said and started to walk toward the cliff track. Wiggins stopped him with a hand on his shoulder.

"No fucking way," the private said. "Besides, you didn't ask nicely."

"And we're going nowhere except back to the chopper until we know what the fuck is going on here," Banks added. He pressed his headset.

"Come and get us," he said.

"I will be right there, Captain," came the reply from the chopper. It swooped in at the other end of the causeway from the pyramid. Banks was watching its approach when the ground beneath him took a lurch, a bigger tremor even than the one they'd faced on the cliff path. The remains of the building nearest them collapsed in on itself as the whole causeway rippled from one end to the other, a wave almost a foot high traveling up the whole length toward the pyramid steps. When the wave hit, the pyramid fell in. The whole structure fell away with a roar and crash of falling masonry, tumbling backward off the ridge and down the cliff, joining the cascade of the waterfall in a fall into the river far below.

The chopper closed in on them but the ground was still bucking and heaving; there was no chance of it making a touchdown. The cabin door slid open, and the co-pilot stood there, letting down a short rope ladder.

"S-Squad, we are leaving," Banks shouted to make himself heard above the din of the chopper's rotors. "Wiggo, get the wanker onto that bird, one way or another. Don't take no for an answer."

He was looking at the chopper, so he didn't see the start of what happened next. He only had the sarge's shocked gaze to tell him that there was still more trouble incoming.

*

He turned to see a huge hole in the hill where the pyramid had been seconds before. The sides, a melee of tumbling worked stone, tree roots, and loose dirt, kept falling inward. The causeway trembled and shook again, almost knocking Banks off his feet, and partially turning him around in the process. The whole ridge on the hilltop bucked and heaved again, and another of the squat buildings tumbled into ruin.

"Wiggo," he shouted, seeing that Buller still hadn't moved. "I told you. Get that fucker into the chopper. We're leaving."

The private finally moved, dragging a still complaining Buller under the whirling rotors toward the door and the hanging ladder. Even then Buller turned back, tried to push away, shouting something that Banks didn't hear. Wiggins put a quick end to it by knocking the man hard on the back of the head with the butt of his weapon, then helping the co-pilot to haul a now slumped and sluggish Buller up and into the cabin. Wiggins turned and gave Banks a thumbs-up.

Banks looked around, trying to find Hynd and McCally. Both men were stood still, staring at the remains of the pyramid.

And at the impossible thing dragging itself up and out of the rubble.

*

To call it a snake would be to deny the magnificence, the majesty of it. The head came up first, even bigger than the cube of the altar room had been on the self-same spot minutes earlier. Two golden eyes, the slits in each pupil fully as big as a man, stared down the causeway directly at the chopper. The mouth opened, showing brilliant white fangs and a flickering tongue that tasted the air as if eager for feeding. The body that rose up below the head was thicker still, 10, thickening to 15, feet wide. It glistened, gold and green and blue and yellow where the sun hit the shimmering scales.

It kept coming out of the hole to wrap around the remains of the pyramid, each slithering coil causing the hilltop ridge to buck. Ground fell in, as if a void had been created underneath them. One of the few remaining buildings to Bank's right tumbled, not into a hole, but over the edge of the cliff, that was itself eroding rapidly, as if the whole hill might be in the process of coming apart.

McCally raised his weapon, but Banks called out to him.

"Leave it, Cally. I've got a feeling we're going to need a

bigger gun. Get to the chopper!"

McCally and Hynd moved to obey, leaving only Banks standing between the snake and the aircraft, which was side on to the beast, not in any position to defend itself against an attack. But for now, the snake was still in the process of pulling itself up and out of the ground, the great coils now entirely obscuring the foundations of the pyramid below it. Banks was more worried about the hill disappearing completely. He struggled to keep his footing as the paved causeway dropped several feet, throwing worked stone and rubble into the air.

"Time to go, Captain," the chopper pilot shouted in his headset. Banks turned, saw that McCally and Hynd were up and inside the chopper, then had to make a grab for the ladder as a hole formed at his feet. He managed to get one hand on the bottom rung, and looked down to see the whole hilltop collapse below him, a swirling cloud of dry dust almost immediately obscuring the view.

McCally and Hynd hauled him aboard as the chopper rose, inches ahead of the dust cloud. Banks was still looking down when the snake's head came up, impossibly fast toward them, and snapped its jaws shut only feet below them. A purple tongue, 12 feet and more long, slid out and tasted, almost tickled, the chopper's landing rails. Banks got his rifle unslung and sent three rounds into the fleshiest part of it, causing the tongue to draw away. The chopper kept rising, clear of the roil and tumble of dust, circling ever higher above what remained of the hill and temple complex, all of which was now little more than a collapsed pile of stone and dirt little higher than the high canopy of the surrounding jungle.

The snake moved through the rubble, its enormous girth and weight demolishing what little was left even further. It seemed to have lost all interest in them now, and was focused on removing all trace of the temple complex from the face of the earth.

"The gold," Buller wailed.

"Should I fire, Captain?" the pilot said at Banks' ear. "We've got enough to give it a fright if nothing else, maybe even enough to take it down."

"Negative," Banks replied. "Get us out of here. I think we've done enough damage for one day."

"My gold," Buller wailed again, as the snake ground down the last of the hill, and with a surge and whoosh of water, the river ran in to wash away what little was left of the hill and temple complex. There was a new bend in the waterway as the chopper took them away downstream, and not a sign that anything else had ever been there.

- 23 -

"What was all that bollocks with the gold melting, Cap?" Wiggins said, shouting to be heard above the rotors.

Banks looked directly at Buller.

"The wanker here said it himself," Banks replied. "Magic. Snake magic. I think somehow the gold and the snake were part of the same thing. And if the wanker here wants to come back and fuck with it again, that's up to him. But we'll be leaving it well alone."

He went up front and was looking out of the window as they passed over the dredger rig. Boitata had come down river with them, her bulk sending a wake crashing across both sides of the river as she surged and with one smooth movement flowed over the facility, crushing it down into little more than bent metal and splinters of wood in a matter of seconds.

By the time the chopper had passed fully overhead, the whole platform was a mass of debris in the water. The pilot banked around to give Buller a final look at his failure.

The last thing they saw was the river god, Boitata, swimming back upstream, the wash from her passing sending more great waves against the bank on either side.

"Time to go home, lads," Banks said, to an array of smiles from the squad.

"Good. I never want to see a snake that size again," Hynd said.

"Funny, that's what your wife said to me," Wiggins replied.

The End

CHECK OUT OTHER GREAT CRYPTID NOVELS

BIGFOOT WAR
by **Eric S. Brown**

Now a feature film from Origin Releasing. For the first time ever, all three core books of the Bigfoot War series have been collected into a single tome of Sasquatch Apocalypse horror. Remastered and reedited this book chronicles the original war between man and beast from the initial battles in Babblecreek through the apocalypse to the wastelands of a dark future world where Sasquatch reigns supreme and mankind struggles to survive. If you think you've experienced Bigfoot Horror before, think again. Bigfoot War sets the bar for the genre and will leave you praying that you never have to go into the woods again.

CRYPTID ZOO
by **Gerry Griffiths**

As a child, rare and unusual animals, especially cryptid creatures, always fascinated Carter Wilde.

Now that he's an eccentric billionaire and runs the largest conglomerate of high-tech companies all over the world, he can finally achieve his wildest dream of building the most incredible theme park ever conceived on the planet...CRYPTID ZOO.

Even though there have been apparent problems with the project, Wilde still decides to send some of his marketing employees and their families on a forced vacation to assess the theme park in preparation for Opening Day.

Nick Wells and his family are some of those chosen and are about to embark on what will become the most terror-filled weekend of their lives—praying they survive.

STEP RIGHT UP AND GET YOUR FREE PASS...

TO CRYPTID ZOO

CHECK OUT OTHER GREAT CRYPTID NOVELS

SWAMP MONSTER MASSACRE
by **Hunter Shea**

The swamp belongs to them. Humans are only prey. Deep in the overgrown swamps of Florida, where humans rarely dare to enter, lives a race of creatures long thought to be only the stuff of legend. They walk upright but are stronger, taller and more brutal than any man. And when a small boat of tourists, held captive by a fleeing criminal, accidentally kills one of the swamp dwellers' young, the creatures are filled with a terrifyingly human emotion—a merciless lust for vengeance that will paint the trees red with blood.

TERROR MOUNTAIN
by **Gerry Griffiths**

When Marcus Pike inherits his grandfather's farm and moves his family out to the country, he has no idea there's an unholy terror running rampant about the mountainous farming community. Sheriff Avery Anderson has seen the heinous carnage and the mutilated bodies. He's also seen the giant footprints left in the snow—Bigfoot tracks. Meanwhile, Cole Wagner, and his wife, Kate, are prospecting their gold claim farther up the valley, unaware of the impending dangers lurking in the woods as an early winter storm sets in. Soon the snowy countryside will run red with blood on TERROR MOUNTAIN.

CHECK OUT ANOTHER GREAT CRYPTID NOVEL!

REPTILIAN
by John Rust

The South Carolina Lizard Man had always been considered a local legend, a way to draw tourists to rural Lee County.

Until a local man shoots and kills the beast.

Jack Rastun, Karen Thatcher, and their team from the Foundation for Undocumented Biological Investigation are called in to collect the Lizard Man's corpse. When they arrive, they find the man who shot it torn apart, and the creature's body gone.

This is only the beginning. More lizard men emerge from the swamps, stalking and killing townspeople. Rastun, Thatcher, and the FUBI wage a desperate battle to try and end the bloody attacks.

But deadly reptilians are not the only threat. A former Marine is convinced the lizard men are part of a vast global conspiracy, and has a plan to deal with them, one that could mean disaster for the entire county.

With thousands of lives at risk, Rastun and Thatcher are faced with a difficult question. Who is more dangerous? Monster or man?